A MASKED MAN, ENEMIES TO LOVERS, DARK
ROMANCE NOVELLA FOR EVERYONE WHO
LOVES A VILLAIN

ONE
MORE
SECRET

ROXANNA C REVELL

One More Secret
A dark romance novella

Roxanna C Revell

For everyone who loves a villain. For the girls who loved, lost and found themselves again. For the downright dark and dirty fantasies that linger in your mind, of men in masks, your boundaries being pushed, and the toe-curling orgasms we all deserve.

You're welcome!
Roxanna xx

Content Warning

Let's be honest with each other. You're here because you like your romance dark, your men morally grey, your smut on page, and to go on a rollercoaster of emotions with your female lead. That's what I write, and I know that's what you love.

If it isn't, then now is the time to step away. No hard feelings, live and let live. We'll do us, and you can do you.

I also respect you enough to give you a heads up in case there are topics you don't want to read, so here goes...

Rachel had sex at the age of fifteen. It's not on page—only referenced. It's not done for effect or shock value, and the little minx completely denies it ever happened. Here in the UK, the age of consent is sixteen, and growing up, most girls I knew had sex before then—including myself, so I've made the situation the same for our FMC because in many cases, it's the norm here.

What else... there's dub-con, violence, hostage situations, guns, awful men you'll want to punch, drug use, alcohol abuse, neglectful parents, attempted rape, threat of murder, and actual unaliving.

There's also a swoon-worthy, possessively gorgeous male lead, and our girl Rachel is a legend.

Before we get started...

I'm a Brit, and I write in British English. I have many readers in the US, and I know many British authors base their stories in America and write in American English, but that's just not for me.

First, when I write my bad guys, I always envision a Guy Ritchie-style cockney villain, so British English is a must. Secondly, this is who I am and how I express my stories. Other than a slightly different writing style and expressions, it's essentially the same language, right? Lastly, it takes me long enough to get my stories written down in my native language, so changing it to American English is just another barrier to finishing a book.

Why am I writing this? Some readers have been known to slate a book for being written in British English, so this is another opportunity for you to step away from the book.

For those of you still game, one of my lovely alpha readers is from the US, and she flagged some words I should clarify.

A deep dive into British English

Pinched = took or stole.

Wanker = well, it's just an insult that rolls nicely off the tongue (also 'a wank' is jerking off).

Flat = apartment.

Stroppy = moody.
Slag = whore.
Flannel = wash cloth.
Hard man = tough guy.
Fit = hot.
Lift = elevator.

If anything else you're unsure about pops up, you can always DM me.

Contents

Chapter One
Rachel

Eight Years Ago

This is my favourite spot. My safe space. Leaning against a concrete balcony overlooking my world from my sixth-floor perch, surrounded by more tower blocks on a shithole of an estate in Hackney, East London.

When it's dark, you can't see the litter on the ground or the graffiti on the walls. Can't smell the piss-stained stairwells from here, either. With all the lights from the surrounding flats shining bright, it could even look pretty.

It doesn't take much to please me.

The best thing about being out here is the noise. Tyres screech—some twat showing off a car he's stolen—police sirens blare, all making up the soundtrack to my life—just the right level of chaos to block out the sounds coming from Mum's room.

When I got back from Shel's half an hour ago, I was greeted by the sound of a headboard banging against a thin wall, followed closely by Kev's wheezing grunt and Mum's exaggerated moans of pleasure.

Going back out wasn't the best option. Most people leave me alone, given who Dad is, but there's always some chancer or smackhead desperate enough to try something. So, I pinched a pack of cigarettes from Mum's bag and came out here. Not that I smoke, but my phone died, and I need something to pass the time.

My first cigarette is nothing more than a cold butt, crushed on the floor, but since they're still at it, I spark up another. A hot rush of nicotine fills my mouth and singes the back of my throat. I hate the taste, but I inhale it deeply before releasing the toxins into the world.

Fucking Kev! I've lost count of how many times he's dumped her. He treats her like shit until she spreads her legs, and then all is forgotten—problem solved.

"What you doin'?"

"Fuckin' hell!" Jumping to the left, away from the unexpected intrusion, I clutch my chest, my heart racing. "Wanker!" I snap, only to grin like an idiot when I face Nate, my neighbour, saviour, and forever crush.

"You make it too easy," he laughs, so confident.

Nate's face should come with a health warning since it's as damaging to my heart as the cigarette between my fingers. Dark hair, blue eyes, and cheekbones high enough that his long lashes almost brush them when he blinks. Seventeen, going on twenty-one, and far too dangerous to be so pretty.

"Give us one." Our balconies are a metre apart, and as he leans toward me, I reciprocate, meeting him halfway. Nate takes the packet, slides a cigarette between his full lips, and then puts the pack in his pocket.

"Oi! They're my mum's."

Smirking, he lights his cigarette, and I watch with envy as he sucks in a drag. "Teach you not to rob them then, won't it?" He cocks his head to the side in challenge, but he should know better than that.

Stepping away, I reach for the door. "Best go buy some more then. See ya."

"The fuck you will." All traces of humour leave his face as he stares me down. Taking the pack from his pocket, he holds it out. "Come get them."

"Nate..." I groan.

"Have I ever let you fall?"

"Just throw them back."

"Just come over here."

Huffing, I lean over the edge, judging the distance to the ground below. I've hopped over the balcony with Nate hundreds of times, and no, he's never let me fall.

"Rachel," he encourages, the softness making my heart skip a beat.

Giving the door to my flat one last glance, I drop my cigarette to the floor, climb onto the chair, press my palm flat against the wall with one hand and grip Nathan's wrist with the other. Jumping, my feet land on the edge of his balcony, and he pulls me into his hard chest.

He holds me, and I let him because, in truth, he's the safest place I know.

"What's going on?" His breath is hot against my scalp.

"Mum and Kev are making up."

His disgusted scoff expresses what his words don't. "Come in for a bit." Nate leads me into his flat, a carbon copy of mine, except that where my mum's in her room fucking her latest loser, his is passed out on the sofa cradling a bottle of vodka.

Neither of us acknowledges the sight—it's nothing new. Stepping into his personal space always sends tingles through my body, even though I know there's no need. I'm fifteen, and Nate works for my dad, a local hardman who would break his legs if he touched me. Dad knows Nate looks out for me; I think he does it on his say-so, but we keep my trips to his room a secret.

I've tried to get Nate to look at me like the boys in class do. Fluttered my dark lashes, locked my deep brown, doe-eyed gaze on his, pushed out my growing tits and flicked my raven locks over my shoulder. He never notices. Never reacts.

Jumping onto his bed, he picks up his laptop. "What do you wanna watch?"

Exhaling the rest of my nerves, I sit down next to him. "You choose."

Chapter Two
Nate

Rachel groans and covers her ears as her mum's final scream vibrates through the walls. Unfortunately, the volume on my laptop can't compete with the performance next door. "Is it over?"

"I should think so," I laugh. "No idea how that fat fuck has so much stamina."

Rach moves her hands away a fraction, listening for signs of an encore, then drops them completely, leaning back against my headboard and exhaling in relief.

Closing her eyes, she takes a few deep breaths before grinning. "Bet they're looking for the fags now." Giggling, her eyes fly open, and for the first time this evening, they're smiling too.

All I can do for the next ten seconds is stare into them, my heart racing, my dick pulsing before I snap myself of it and focus on the laptop. Rachel is off limits—for more reasons than one. She'll be sixteen in two months, but not yet being legal is the least of my worries. Tony, her dad, has made my role in her life very clear—have her back, but keep my hands off.

I'd do anything for Tony—have done many things for him. He got banged up when Rachel was five and was released four years later, but the damage was done. Rachel's mum, Trish, convinced the courts that he needed to be kept away, going so far as to change their last name. Rachel Cannock became Rachel Taylor, but she never stopped being her father's daughter.

They have their moments—many more than Trish is aware of. He ensures she has what she needs, and I'm here to inform him of what happens in that flat. I'm not betraying Rachel—she knows the deal. I've always been her friend, but Tony gave me a chance when I was nothing more than a scrawny fourteen-year-old, thieving what I could to afford to keep the gas on when Mum drank the last of our funds.

It's been easy to stick to the rules because Tony has my loyalty, and up until a year ago, Rachel was like a little girl. That's changed now. She has my attention even when she's not trying, which she is more and more.

"Is it really that good?"

Swallowing hard to bring myself back to the moment, I tilt my head to the side to find Rachel staring straight ahead, her cheeks flushed. "What?"

Turning to me, her face burns even brighter. "You know... sex?"

My dick stands tall as she utters the word, and I clear my throat. "What? Yeah... No... Why the fuck are you asking? Are you seeing someone?"

"What? No, calm the fuck down," she mocks. "I just... it just seems to solve all their problems," she shrugs, nodding to the wall.

Slamming the laptop closed, I sit up straight. "Sex doesn't solve problems, Rach." Staring at her, I hold her gaze, trying to gauge what's going through her head.

"Seems to make Mum happy," she shrugs. "The girls in my class—"

"No," I snap, and she gapes in response. "Look... I don't want to talk about this with you."

"Why? Because the thought of someone wanting me is so ridiculous to you?" Pain radiates from her eyes, so raw, it tears through my gut. "Fuck this." Rach swings her legs off the bed, but I grab her arm before she can get up and keep her in place.

"Don't go back there," I grit out. "I don't like you being around Kev." Shoving the laptop aside, I pull her legs back onto the bed, holding her closer to me than before. "You can stay with me." A little longer... that's what I should've said, but that's not what I want. I want her to stay exactly where she is all night so I can keep her safe. Shield her from the shit in that flat and her head.

"I don't want to cramp your style," she huffs. "You could have any girl you want here. It's not like I've not heard you before."

"Shit... Rach..." I shake my head. These crappy flats and their thin walls. I'm seventeen, for fuck's sake, and the girls around here make it easy. "I'm—"

"Why can't it be me?" she whispers, completely flooring me.

My mouth hangs open, and my brain's unable to form words.

"Why?"

"You know why," I choke out.

"You think I'm ugly." Tears light up her eyes—all this pain is my doing, and yet I don't know how we got here.

"You're not ugly, Rachel. You're fifteen, and your dad would kill me," I argue.

Watching me for a moment, she inhales a deep breath. "Sooo... you think I'm pretty?"

Running a hand over my closely shaven hair, I force the words, ready to dart out, back down my throat. "We can't talk like this."

"It's just a question."

"With an answer that will cost me my kneecaps!" I glare at her, but all she does is smile.

"That's a yes then," she beams like all her Christmases came at once.

Sighing, I cup her chin, holding her in place. "I'm going to say this once... that's it, and it stays our secret."

Maintaining eye contact, she gives a slight nod—no intention of pulling away from my hold.

"You're fit as fuck, Rachel."

She bursts out laughing at my bluntness, her cheeks… her chest flushing.

"I'm not blind, OK? So please stop making being around you harder than it already is."

Holding my gaze, her lips part, and she sucks in a breath. "I'm nearly sixteen."

"Rach…" I groan.

"You already hide things from him," she pushes.

Him. Tony. Yes, I keep the fact that our film nights take place in my room, alone, from him, but I do so knowing I've never touched her.

Rachel presses her palm against my hand, her eyes claim mine, and it's all I can do to keep myself grounded as she asks, "What's one more secret?"

Chapter Three
Trish

I'm going to kill her!

I'm going to make sure she's OK, then I'm going to kill her.

It's 7:45 am on Friday, and Rachel's nowhere to be seen. She came home from Shel's, left her schoolbag, dead phone, and keys here—that part I know, but what came next is any fucker's guess.

Pacing the room, I check her now-charging mobile, trying to get clues from the incoming notifications. Nothing. I should've realised she wasn't here, but it was only after Kev left that I checked her room—ten minutes ago. I know well enough that the police won't be bothered. Anyway, I can guess where to look first.

Grabbing my shoes, I head to the door only to be stopped by two loud knocks. Yanking it open, I gasp,

"Jesus fucking Christ!" Gripping a sheepish-looking Rachel by her school shirt, I pull her in and give her the once-over.

"Chill out! I'm fine." The stroppy little madam has the audacity to look put out.

"Where have you been?"

"Literally right next door." She points to the wall to her left like it's no big deal.

"You…" I clear my throat and attempt to slow my racing heart. "You slept with Nathan?"

She turns away from me, a bad sign, and stomps to her room. "As in, I fell asleep there… Yes, Mum."

"Rachel—"

"I'm going to get ready for school."

Storming behind, I yank her back, forcing her to face me. "Where did you sleep?"

Scoffing, she shakes her head, eyes darting to the floor. "I didn't mean to freak you out or fall asleep. It just happened."

"Look at me."

"I'm going to be late."

"Look. At. Me."

Reluctantly, she does as I ask, her eyes full of venom.

When did it come to this? We used to be close… she was my baby girl. She's not been a baby for a long time. She's a young woman on the verge of God only knows what, too gorgeous for her own good and too fucking stubborn for mine. Staring at her, I try to tell what else has changed, but her widening eyes prompt me to speak.

"Where did you sleep?" I ask more calmly. Leaning closer, I catch a distinctly male scent, and fear takes hold of me.

She sees it. "It's not what you think! We were on his bed watching a film, and we fell asleep. That's it."

"Liar." I almost choke on the word.

"Oh, fuck off, I don't need this right now."

"Rachel… you're fifteen."

"And how old were you when you got with Dad?" she rages, going on the attack, taking the attention off herself. I know how this girl works.

"You don't need to make the same mistakes as m—"

"Oh… so you're saying I'm a slag and a mistake? Thanks a fucking bunch!"

"No! I'm saying that I know better now, and you don't—"

"You know better?" she yells. "It didn't sound like that last night." Shoving past me, she stalks to her door, only to spin around and charge right back to me. "If I did have sex last night—which I didn't, who would be to blame, hey?"

Her words land exactly as intended, right in the centre of my heart.

"Now it's Kev; before that, it was Tommy; before him, it was Sean; before Sean, it was who-the-fuck-even-remembers-anymore. It doesn't matter what they're called because it's always the same. You fight, you fuck, everything's lovely, you're in control, so you fuck some more until they tire of you!"

Tears burn the back of my eyes, and on seeing them, Rachel's eyes glisten, too. Despite what she's just said, she loves me. She's just trying to take the focus off herself.

Forcing out a long breath, I step closer—I can't let this go. "Tell me the truth."

Snorting a bitter laugh, she moves away from me, her face full of contempt. "Everything I know about relationships, I learned from you. That's the truth, Mum. Make of that what you will."

Rachel left for school four hours ago. All I've done for those four hours is stare at the wall, playing her words on repeat. She probably thought they'd hurt me, and then I'd let my anger win and brush them off.

I haven't. I can't.

It's like she's stapled a mirror to my forehead, and I'm forced to stare at my reflection—my past. I'm seeing the events of the last seventeen years on repeat, the pattern that started with Tony and then continued after he left.

It's not the number of men she threw in my face that's eating at me; it's just three of the many vile words she spewed—you're in control.

Is that what she thinks? I was in control... That sex gave me power.

Sex gave me nothing but a momentary reprieve from the rest of their bullshit. I've never been in control of shit, but I'm going to get control of this situation, just as soon as I figure out how. My first thought was to take a rolling pin next door and batter Nate with it until he confesses what he did. Then I thought getting Tony to do it would hurt him more. I almost called him, but stopped when I realised that Rachel would hate me for it.

Now I'm pondering my last option. The only one that truly gives me control—cutting my losses and getting the hell away from this place. I moved here with Tony and stayed because I couldn't admit defeat to my parents back home in Nottingham. My job pays the bills, but that's all it does; Kev will soon be gone, and Rachel gets closer to ruining her life every single day.

There's nothing to keep us here—no real reason to stay.

It takes another hour, three cigarettes and two coffees before I'm buzzing enough to overcome my nerves. I'm about to do what I swore I never would, but whilst contemplating my disaster of a life, I've realised there's only one thing to do, for my daughter and myself... I need to leave it all behind.

Phone in my shaking hand, I swallow down the last of my nerves and make the call, and on three rings, she answers. "Hello, Trish."

Mum. My heart races, and I force the dread back down. We've rebuilt our relationship over the years, but the lost time—the regret remains.

"You alright, love?" she asks, her Midlands accent, thick as ever, homely as ever.

"Actually, Mum... there's something I need to talk to you about."

"Is it Rachel?" she panics. "Is she OK?"

"She's fine..." A sob rips from my throat, the pain of the day too much to contain. "No, really... she's OK, Mum. Don't worry."

"Trish..." Mum sighs. "Are you OK?"

"I will be... I... We..." Shit. Why is this so hard? "Mum... can I please come home?"

Chapter Four
Rachel

Present Day

My laptop hums, overheating as it attempts to download a much-needed update. I barely hear it as I stare out my window, watching people clutching their umbrellas while they grab whatever they need on their lunch break. Not me. As much as I hate feeling caged in my office, I'll stay exactly where I am.

I can't stand the rain. It reminds me of the worst day of my life.

Eight years ago, give or take a week or two, Mum picked me up from school with a bag full of clothes, telling me we needed a weekend away. Naturally, I resisted wanting to spend my weekend with someone else. So, she used her 'ace', telling me my beloved Grandad was sick, and I unwittingly hopped on a train to Nottingham.

When Sunday evening rolled by, and she announced I could pull a sickie for a few days off school, I remembered why I loved her. Two days later, a van arrived with all our belongings, and she informed me that we were leaving London for good.

To say I lost my shit is an understatement.

I ran to the local train station, ignoring the rain slamming down on me, stinging and freezing my exposed skin. I didn't care that the London train didn't stop there. I just needed to get home. Grandad showed up in his car and coaxed me inside, and I followed, more to escape the rain than anything else.

Grandad Dennis was the peacekeeper... I miss him. He did his best to explain why Mum had uprooted my entire life, taking me away from the people I was already dying to get back to. I didn't understand, not for months, but the longer those I mourned remained away, doing nothing to fight for me, not even answering my calls or replying to my texts, the less inclined I was to waste my energy on heartbreak.

Suppressing my nature—the side of me that proved I was my father's daughter, I decided to live this better life Mum promised me. I became a muted image of my true self—a safer version where bad boys with pretty faces couldn't ever hurt me again.

Nate disappeared from my life, but Dad kept in touch, even visited occasionally. As I got older and more resentful of the life and people he prioritised over me, I let things slide until I barely made contact beyond birthdays and Christmas.

It didn't stop me rushing to London on my eighteenth birthday. Dad had begged me to come and celebrate with him and was waiting for me with open arms. I felt like I belonged there, a little girl shielded by a dangerous man who made my world safe and allowed me to be myself.

He took me to his local pub, and everything came crashing down. It was foolish to hope it would be different, that seeing me in person would pique his interest again. It didn't. Nate's arms were full, his hands too busy groping some girl to even glance at me. He was completely embedded in my dad's way of life and everything it involved.

Come to think of it... that was the worst day of my life. After Dad's initial warmth, it was clear I was in the way—that Nate was more a son than I ever would be a daughter. The wall I built, which I thought was impenetrable, crumbled, but my heart turned to steel.

"Are you free?" Dan's voice snaps me out of my memories. "I did knock," he offers.

He probably did. "It depends on what you need. My laptop's got that Friday feeling."

Dan smiles sheepishly, closes the door, and I instantly regret being so accommodating. Dan is the manager of this nightclub. I've not quite figured out the hierarchy since I'm the HR Manager for the three clubs we have in this region. It wouldn't usually matter to me, but I feel it's about to become relevant.

"Are you having drinks with us after work?" he asks, fiddling with the photo frame on my desk.

Walking over to it, I sit and reposition the photo of the Twinsies to where it's supposed to be. "I can't tonight, I'm babysitting."

"Your sisters?"

Sisters—I never thought I'd have them, but two years after leaving London, Mum met Johnson; they fell madly in love, married, and produced Bella and Ivy—also known as the Twinsies. For once, Mum did things right—picked a good one—and it helps that he's dirt-rich, even if his parents are arseholes.

"What are you doing tomorrow?" he asks, swallowing hard.

Here we go. It's my fault. I know better than to mix business and pleasure, but his persistence and my boredom made me cave. "I'm babysitting."

"All weekend?" he challenges.

"All weekend." Thanks to Mum and Johnson for extending their holiday. The twins have been with their doting Grandparents all week—theirs, not mine—but they have plans all weekend, so big sis has been asked to step up.

Dan's expression darkens, thinking I'm making an excuse when, for once, I'm being completely genuine. "I thought we could go out sometime."

Sitting forward, I rest my elbows on my desk, place my chin in my hands and gaze at him. "Why?"

Clearing his throat, Dan shuffles on his feet. "Why?" He shakes his head. "Rach, we've spent the last four Fridays having amazing sex. I thought we could take the next step."

'Amazing' is an overstatement.

Leaning back, I sigh as if this conversation will be difficult. My time in HR has taught me how to appear empathetic, whether it's genuine or not. "Dan... I thought I was clear that it was just fun... just sex."

Just sex. It's always just sex.

When life broke my heart, I made a vow to myself. Nobody would have the power to hurt me again. Nobody would ever get close enough to make me feel unworthy—forgettable. I call the shots. I keep control.

Dan's face reddens, and he leans back on his heels awkwardly. "Yeah... but then we kept doing it, so I thought..." Catching my blank expression, he changes tack. "I guess not." Scoffing, his eyes darken. "Wow... you're a real bitch."

"A bitch?" My eyebrows shoot to the ceiling, but I keep my cool. It's not the first time I've had my rules on casual sex thrown in my face, but it pisses me off all the same. "I was straight with you from the start, Dan. Sex doesn't always lead to feelings. That's no different just because I'm female, and you know fucking well that if I were a bloke, you'd be patting me on the back."

Rounding my desk, I walk to the door and hold it open for him.

He strides towards me, pushes the door closed and gets in my face. "I can make life here hell for you. You know that, right?"

"What I know, Dan, is that I have the trust and respect of Kim, our recently divorced HR Director, *who's just itching for an opportunity to reclaim her power."*

Dan's chest heaves, his rage barely contained.

Takes a bit more than that to scare me. Leaning closer, I whisper, "I'd hate to have to report you for sexual harassment."

Chapter Five
Rachel

"Rach!" my best friend squeals, making the speakers of my VW Polo vibrate. "What time are you coming over?"

"Tash…" I chastise, rolling my eyes. "Did you not read my message?"

"I did, but I was hoping it was a joke." She exhales dramatically. "The whole weekend… why are they so fucked up?"

They, as in my rich and pretentious step-grandparents.

A smile spreads across my face. This is the one person I can be almost my whole self with. I met Natasha six months after we moved here, when she decided to plough through the invisible barricade I erected around myself. It was a school day—

lunchtime; she was next to me in the queue, but I didn't notice her until she grabbed my elbow and guided me to an empty table.

"I just want you to know that I can help," she'd said, her face full of concern.

"With what?" I'd stuttered in response.

"With whatever is… You know… happening."

Even in my confusion, her dramatic expressions made me smile inside. "What do you think's happening?"

"Well…" She lowered her head, checking our surroundings. "If you're being hurt—"

"Woah!" Knocking my drink over, all eyes on us, I used my sleeve to wipe up the mess while frantically whispering, "You've got it so wrong. Nothing's happening to me. I promise."

Tasha stared at me for a whole minute, and I squirmed under the intensity of her all-seeing gaze until she broke the silence in the best possible way: "Then why are you such a miserable loner?"

It was the first time I'd laughed in months, and we've been best friends since. She was a rock, loving, loyal, and consistent—she still tells it like it is.

So do I. "Yes, well, their social life is more important than mine, and they have been put upon all week," I emphasise the words Grace, the twins' grandmother, had spoken when she called me this morning.

"Puh-lease, she loves spoiling them," Tash scoffs before sighing in defeat. She knows it's a done deal. "Dinner on Monday." It wasn't a question.

"Absolutely."

Rush-hour traffic slows me down, making what should be a ten-minute journey almost double. It's odd that neither Grace nor Jeremy has called to complain that I'm late—they usually would, but I'll take the win.

Grace and Jeremy have always been shitty with me—Mum, too. They only accepted her after she gave birth to their grandchildren. Johnson, their only child, married beneath him—I overheard them telling their friends at a party. They knew I heard, but didn't care, because that's who the Parkers are—pretentious twats with more money than they deserve.

Mum knew how they felt. She barely had a penny to her name when they met, and then there was me— the excess baggage. Thankfully, Johnson isn't a dick like his parents. He saw a woman who worked hard for all she had. A mother who had moved heaven and earth to give me a better life.

She wasn't wrong. My life is better than it would've been if we stayed in London. My heart was drawn to the things that would ruin me, things I still miss, which is another reason I keep it closed for business.

No need to open that wound. Besides, Tasha and the twins help ease the monotony.

As for Grace and Jeremy, since I'm not into sharing with my Mum and can't give them grandchildren, I have no chance of winning them over.

"Bleurgh!" Gagging at the thought, I settle on something that gives me genuine glee—they now have to ask their son for access to their money because Jeremy gambled so much of it away.

Not that I'm supposed to know that.

Pulling up to the cast iron gates guarding their two-acre garden, which is also fully walled and lined by massive oak trees, I lower my window and reach across to buzz the intercom. They can see me on the camera, but will still expect me to announce myself. So, I keep the window low, the cool breeze gently whipping around my neck and sending chills down my spine. I probably should've changed out of my V-neck camel jumper dress before heading here, but that would've only made me later.

Shivering a little, I wait for the voice, only to jump when the gate releases with a buzz and opens. Immobile, I stare at the silent intercom, stunned. That's a first.

Pulling forward, I stop when I clear the gates and wait for them to close behind me before slowly making *my way up the drive to the hidden house. As soon as it comes into view, nerves creep into my gut. My past—my dad—has made me pretty formidable, but as beautiful as this house is, I never feel welcome. It has no soul, like its owners. Thankfully, the twins will be waiting by the door, shoes on and cases packed.*

Bracing myself, I leave my coat and bag in the car and jog to the door, finger raised, ready to ring the bell…

There's no need.

The door is open, just an inch. An invitation that makes me question my sanity. I'd like to say this is a sign of trust, but if anything, Grace is probably just too busy to wait for me. Charming.

"It's just me… Rachel," I call, lightly knocking as I step inside. They may have left it open, but Grace has snapped at me before for wandering in.

Silence. No sisters waiting for me. No sounds of Grace hurrying Jeremy along. This is not the norm nor convenient—I was hoping to spend as little time here as possible.

Clearing my throat, I call out again. "Grace. Jeremy… I'm here."

Nothing.

Fuck's sake.

Closing the front door, I notice the sound of the TV in the background and walk towards the living room. The door's closed, so I knock before opening it wide out of habit.

Empty again... but not silent, thanks to the TV.
"Twinsies..." I call in my mock stern voice. "Are you
hiding?"

A giggle breaks loose from behind the sofa before
being quickly stifled, and my heart rate returns to a
steady pace—this whole thing is starting to creep me
out. "Hmmm..." I tiptoe towards the sofa. "I guess if
nobody's here, I should just go home and eat all the ice
cream my—"

"BOO!"

"Shit!" I yell, before slamming my hand over my
mouth.

Bella and Ivy burst into hysterics, falling all over
the sofa.

"Rachie said a bad word," Ivy snorts.

Bending over, I take a deep breath and get myself
together. I was expecting them to jump out, but the
masks surprised me. "Where are these from?" I poke
them both in the ribs before getting a closer look at the
pink bunny masks covering the top half of their faces—
not their grandparents' usual style.

Shaking off the last of their laughter, Ivy sits up
and wraps an arm around my shoulder. "They're part
of the game."

Lifting the mask, I look into her bright blue eyes,
sparkling with mischief. "And what game is that?"

"I can explain the rules."

My spine straightens, my body rigid, like all the air
has been sucked from my lungs. My knees almost
buckle, but the sofa keeps me upright. In a split second,
the mood in the room turns from carefree to crippling

fear—only mine though. Belly and Ivy still have smiles on their faces, but that man... whoever just spoke shouldn't be here—that I know, and it has every nerve in my body alive and ready for battle.

Taking a deep breath, I edge along the sofa, ensuring my sisters are behind me, and turn. The inhaled breath leaves me in a ragged gasp, and my arms spread wide, shielding the twins further.

The game... the masks... he's wearing one, too, only his is black and silver, more Donny Darko than Bugs Bunny. It covers his head as if sewn into a bandana, leaving everything below his nose visible.

"Who the fuck are you?" *I force out, hoping I can cover my fear.*

He smiles and points to his hoodie, bringing my gaze to the only part of his clothing that isn't black—a white number one.

"He's One," *Bella announces as if this is all completely normal.*

"Get back," *I hiss.*

"Now, now." *The man—One—steps closer.* "We're all friends here, Rachel."

East London. I'd know the accent anywhere.

Remember everything. "You need to leave... Just walk away," *I grind out.*

Now mere inches from my body, he rests his hands across his stomach. So calm in comparison to my shaking limbs. "I'm afraid we can't do that."

"We?"

"One, Two and Three fell out of a tree!" *Ivy sings, causing Bella to fall back down in hysterics.*

Instead of hushing them, I remain frozen, eyes locked on One's lips—the only part of him that looks human. "Three?" I whisper, gasping when another thought slams into my mind. "Where are Grace and Jeremy?"

"Rachel..." One's right hand slowly moves towards my face, his fingers grazing my cheek as he guides a strand of hair behind my ear. I ignore the burn, the sense of Déjà vu. I don't look for what's familiar. He's the rabbit, but I'm the deer frozen in the headlights.

"I told you. We're all friends here, and it will stay that way as long as everyone plays their part." One stares at me, his eyes exploring my face like he's cataloguing every freckle and crease. "Come." He steps back, gesturing for me to follow. "It's time to learn the rules."

"I'm not leaving my sisters alone." This time I don't have to pretend. The strength in my voice is real, even if I don't stand a chance. One's got over a foot on me in height and looks to be about four times my body weight—and who knows about the other two. Still, if they touch Ivy or Bella, I'll gouge their eyes out before they can even blink.

Ignoring me, One addresses my sisters. "Girls... How much fun have we had this afternoon?" he asks, his playful tone contrasting with his appearance.

Bella bounces on the sofa, something she'd never usually do. "Loads and loads and loads!" she squeals.

"Grandma and Grandad haven't stopped us from doing anything," Ivy offers, joining her sister for a cushion fight.

All afternoon. These fuckers have been here all afternoon, and the only way the girls wouldn't be told off for their behaviour is because Grace and Jeremy haven't been able to.

As if reading my mind, One takes my hand and walks me towards the door. "You girls stay here. Understand?"

I don't hear their reply, but I know they'll do as he says. One is in control here; there's no doubt about that. The girls will listen in the same way I'm following—complying. I couldn't pull my hand from his if I tried. Every step he takes towards the kitchen, he grips it tighter, the beat of our pulses just as strong and fast—maybe he's not so calm after all.

The second the thought enters my head, a hand clamps over my mouth as I'm spun around and slammed into the wall, held in place, dwarfed by One's body pressing against mine. Releasing my hand, he places one palm flat against the wall, keeping the other firmly across my lips.

Lowering his head, his eyes come level with mine, and I get a good look at them for the first time. Blue... but not clear and bright. More like the traces of blue that remain visible when the sky is full of dark grey clouds waiting to break into a storm.

"You weren't supposed to be here," he whispers, his breath brushing my cheeks, fanning me in an addictive warmth. Despite his rage—or worry, I can't decide which, I'm not afraid. Something about One feels safe, familiar… inviting.

Maybe it's because the girls were so calm? It has to be. The alternative is way too fucked up. Even with the freaky bunny mask covering half his face, One's full lips and chiselled jaw hint at what he's concealing. Those eyes… the small glimpse I'm getting, revealing a sliver of his soul—dark, unyielding, possessive.

Addictive.

Something about this whole thing reminds me of home. Our flat back in London, the people, the smells, the danger lurking in the stairwells at night.

The thought is sobering, the risk is real, but there's no time to make any sense of it because on my next intake of breath, I'm yanked towards the kitchen.

Chapter Six
Nate

Five hours ago

"*Boss... we have a situation.*" *I choose my words carefully. It's a change in circumstances, not a problem. To call it an issue suggests it's beyond my control, and it's not.*

"*Talk to me,*" *Boss replies. His calmness down to his trust in me, his confidence in my abilities.*

"*The holiday has been extended. They're back Sunday morning.*" *I pause for him to speak, but he doesn't.* "*The old couple have fallen in line. They've cancelled all their plans for the weekend, but it won't be just them and the kids.*"

That gets his attention. "We have a party crasher?"

"Yes…" This pause is for me to breathe deeply over my churning gut. "They already asked the kids' older sister to pick them up. She's due to arrive this evening."

"Their sister?" he hums low, his voice gritty. We're well aware of her existence, but she has no part to play in our plans. "Tell them to cancel her."

Oh, I did. Not an option, apparently. "The old woman suggested that cancelling would lead to questions. If they say they're ill—same shit they told their friends—she'll come and get the kids anyway."

Boss remains silent for another minute while the cogs twist this new information around his mind. The wait is as long as the lump in my throat is heavy, but finally, he sighs. "Rachel's joining the game, after all."

Rachel. I thought not speaking her name would somehow make it not real. Fuck it. We are where we are. The kids' big sister is Rachel—Boss' Rachel… and mine.

"You keep Two and Three in line. Understood?"

Two and Three—Vic and Jonno—great for instilling fear, usually smart enough to know I'm Boss's right-hand and what I say goes, even if they're only hired help and not part of our crew. They were a good choice for the job when it was little kids and pensioners, but Rachel changes things.

The plan was to use the kids to keep the grandparents obedient, and when dear Mummy and Daddy got back, they'd have no choice but to do our bidding. Rachel's a spare part who happens to be hot as sin. They'll see her as fair game unless I intervene. "You should speak to them."

"And risk them guessing how we're connected," he barks. "They take the money and do the job, but Rachel isn't part of the agreement."

No. To them, she'll be a perk of it—something to use and abuse. Destroy.

My lunch threatens to come back up. "I understand."

"Do you?" *Boss grinds out before releasing a deep sigh.* "You know how they work."

"I'll stake my claim on her." *Stepping out of the front door, so the men in question can't hear me, I walk the perimeter of the house.*

"Your claim?" *Boss laughs bitterly.* "Words mean nothing to them. They'll only respect your claim if—"

"If what?" *I spit. I know where this is going, and it tastes fucking nasty.*

"Nate," *Boss exhales, breaking our rules about using real names.* "What will you do when they touch her?"

When. Not if because these pricks have form.

"I'll chop their dicks off and feed them to them before cutting their fucking hearts out!" *Ain't that the absolute truth?*

I stayed away from Rachel all these years because she deserved a better life—a normal existence where she could settle down and spend her weekends going on long walks instead of dodging bullets.

That doesn't mean anything's changed.

"Shit's in motion." Boss lets the words sink in, my racing heartbeat sending them straight to my blackened soul. "You can't kill them, not yet anyway, and you can't protect Rachel unless you make her yours."

Dragging my nails against my mask, the cheap polyester irritating my freshly shaven skin, not quite believing this conversation is happening. "We're talking about your daughter, here."

"We're talking about my baby!" he yells, before taking several deep breaths in. "She wasn't supposed to be part of this, but we're in too deep to walk away. You've always done what it takes to keep her safe. Do what needs to be done now."

Chapter Seven
Rachel

One pushes the kitchen door open, and I scrunch my free hand into a fist to stop it from shaking. Air fills my lungs, and then it stays there, frozen as I take in the sight before me. Grace and Jeremy sit at the kitchen table, side by side, hands flat on the oak top, eyes low. On the outside, she looks immaculate—like always—but the air of confidence that usually radiates from her, that makes her brighter, is nowhere to be seen.

She looks almost grey. Jeremy, on the other hand, is white as the marble top that fills the plush, high-end kitchen.

Releasing my breath, I dare to take in the rest of the room; my eyes zoning straight in on the two people who shouldn't be here—Two and Three, according to their hoodies. Dressed exactly like One—all in black, freaky rabbit mask, and numbered accordingly. Two meets my gaze, his cloaked eyes giving nothing away, but his sneer tells me all I need to know, and my body recoils on instinct.

Two's shorter than One and broader, but it looks more like fat than muscle.

Remember everything… Accents, size, mannerisms, and teeth. When this is over, I need to give the police as much as possible.

I focus on Three next, similar in height to Two but much leaner. All three are clean-shaven, giving as little as possible away.

Pressure against my lower back snaps my attention to One, who guides me towards the kitchen table. Pulling out the chair opposite Grace and Jeremy, he places a hand on my shoulder, forcing me to sit.

"Rachel, meet Two and Three."

Turning, I nod slightly, my instincts warning me that it's best to play nice—for now.

"Two and Three, this is Rachel."

Two steps forward, my eyes widen in horror as he reaches out his gloved hand in greeting. Saliva pools in my mouth at the thought of him making contact. I don't want to piss them off, but I can't have him near me. One's dangerous, but the vibes Two and Three give off make me want to claw my way out of my skin.

My mouth opens, my throat constricts, but before Two can get any closer, One's large hand wraps around his wrist, locking it in place. "Look," he grinds out, "but don't fucking touch."

Three steps closer, a silent standoff forming, Two and Three together—One alone. I get the feeling he'd beat them regardless, but it's not a dynamic that brings me comfort: Two and Three have each other's backs.

One releases Two's wrist and places both hands on my shoulders, a move that feels both possessive and protective. Why don't I recoil from him?

"I don't think keeping our new arrival in suspense any longer is fair. Do you, Grace?"

Grace jumps when One speaks her name, finally acknowledging my presence with a weak smile. I offer none in return.

"I'll be honest, Rachel." One sits beside me. "Things haven't gone to plan." Smiling, he manages to give the sense that he's unfazed. "Your mum and stepdad were due earlier today; when they arrived here, we'd be waiting; your stepdad would feel compelled to do as we ask, and then we'd be on our merry way."

My stomach lurches at the thought of Mum facing this shit without me.

"As you can see, things have changed," One chuckles. "So, we'll need to trespass on Grace and Jeremy's hospitality a little longer."

"Nice house," Three speaks up in an accent I can't place. Not local, but not London either. "Good company," he adds.

If he looks at me when he speaks, I've no idea, but One twists his body closer. The tension radiating from him, combined with Grace and Jeremy's fear—and mine for the two oblivious girls in the living room—swirls around my head. It's dizzying...

Gritting my teeth, I stare straight at One. "What is it that you need Johnson to do?"

One tilts his head… I wish I could see his face so I could figure him out. "Access a bank account. If we know about Jeremy's troubles…" One pauses to glare at the man in question. "I'm sure you do, too. Johnson is the only one who can make a transfer, and holding his parents and children hostage would be his incentive to do as he's told."

Money… of course. "And once that's done?" I ask, my heart pounding.

"Then we leave, and you can all get on with your lives." One maintains eye contact, no suggestion of a lie.

It feels too easy. "Just like that?"

"Poof!" Three announces, emphasising the sound with his hands. "Gone without a trace."

Why I push, I'm not sure, maybe I need to know exactly how bad things will get. Turning my gaze to Three, I add, "Except for the transfer trail, and the police—"

"Ah… the police." One scrunches his nose in distaste. "You're not going to call the police, are you?" He turns his attention to Grace and Jeremy, who shake their heads in unison.

What the fuck have they done to make them so scared?

"You see, Rach…" Rach… it rolls off his tongue like he's known me forever. "The tax man doesn't know this particular account exists, and Grace, Jeremy and your stepdaddy would be fucked if he did."

Staring at Grace and Jeremy, my mouth hangs open in shock. I knew they were greedy, but I thought they had too high an opinion of themselves to break the law.

"So," One continues. "As long as you three do as you're told until Sunday morning, and you keep those girls calm so we don't have any extra hassle, there's no reason we can't all get along."

Exhaling deeply, I close my eyes. Two nights. We'll have to make it through two nights with three potential psychos... Who've been alone with my sisters. "Tell me..." I grind out, hiding my shaking hands under the table. "What game have you been playing with those two five-year-old girls?"

"Steady on," Two laughs. "Got a dirty mind, this one."

Ignoring him, I stare at One, who seems unfazed by my rising anger. "We've called it Five Bunnies Rule the Burrow."

"Meaning we've let the spoiled brats do whatever they want," Two clarifies.

"Which was acceptable, for three hours," One continues. "But you're going to need to help rein them in from now on."

It's a slight relief, knowing my sisters have probably had the best day of their lives, but they're five, and they will soon get bored. Which means they'll cause problems.

"Where's your phone, Rachel?" One asks, snapping me from visions of what's to come.

Keeping my eyes closed, I reply. "In the car."

"Keys?"

Opening them, I shrug in defeat. "In the car."

One nods over my shoulder, and Two leaves the room. "Is anyone expecting to see you this weekend, Rachel?"

"Yes... wait... no," I stutter.

One's warm fingers grip my chin, holding me in place as he stares me down. "Which is it?"

"No," I answer confidently. "I did have plans. I cancelled them to have the girls."

"Boyfriend?" he asks, his voice thick.

"No... my best friend." Pulling back, I try to release myself, hating what his tone is doing to my body, but he grips tighter.

"Do you have a boyfriend, Rachel?" One's voice is seductive yet deadly, a combination that makes goosebumps spread across my covered arms.

"That's none of your business," I bite back, fighting my reaction to him.

"Grace..." One's eyes remain on mine, burning into me, making every part of me overheat. "Does Rachel have a boyfriend?"

I try to turn in her direction, but One holds me in place.

"O-oh..." she replies nervously. "No... not that I'm aware."

One releases a deep breath, his Adam's apple bobs, and I again feel dizzy and so very out of control.

"Here." Two holds my bag above my head—I didn't even hear him return.

Exhaling deeply, I welcome Two's interruption, taking Ones' heat and attention from me. One releases my chin and takes my bag, tipping the contents onto the table, not caring if there's anything in there that might embarrass me, like the open pack of condoms.

Three chuckles behind me, but One scoops them up and slips them into the pocket of his hoodie.

Fuck! Straightening my shoulders, I try to act like I don't care, but I've never felt so vulnerable.

Picking up my phone, One's eyes lock on mine, his jaw tense like he's grinding his teeth. "Password," *he demands, much colder than before, and my hand instinctively reaches out to touch the screen with my thumb.*

"No. The passcode, not your fingerprint."

Clearing my throat, I take a second to accept that this man is about to get a front-row seat to my entire life, and there's nothing I can do about it. "Two, eight, zero, four."

One's fingers move as I speak, freezing for a second on the last number. My screen lights up, but his eyes remain fixed on me. "What do those numbers mean to you?"

Everything. "Nothing," *I lie.* "Just a random combination."

Turning his attention to my phone, he goes to my messages to confirm my story. Setting my phone aside, he tips his head towards Jeremy and Grace, a devilish grin on his face. "Tasha doesn't like you two much, does she?"

"She telling the truth?" Two asks, still standing way too close to me.

"It appears so." One slides my phone into the same pockets as the condoms, causing my cheeks to flush bright red.

I'm not usually embarrassed. I'm single, and if I want to have sex with someone, I do it safely. Still, with these three surrounding me, it feels like an open invitation I never intended to send. I'm utterly exposed and entirely at their mercy.

Two clears his throat, and an alarm blares inside my head, warning me I won't like what he says. So, like the sucker for punishment, I am, I stare right at him.

Does he ever not smirk?

Two's curled lips part. "What about the—"

"Who's hungry?" One interrupts, and right on cue, my stomach growls. "There's everything you need to make spaghetti bolognese." One stands up, his hand outstretched to me. "Time to make yourself useful."

The bluntness in his voice causes a chill to slide down my sweaty spine. In a fucked-up way, One felt like an ally—the lesser evil, but that changed in the blink of an eye. I must remember that even though they keep throwing the word around, we are not friends. They're here to take.

Standing, I follow him to the fridge. "I would ask Grace, but she was shaking so much when she made a cuppa earlier that she scolded herself. If I give her a knife, she might lose a limb and bleed to death."

"Which would be inconvenient," Three laughs.

I can tell them apart without turning. Two's voice is deep and gruff, and Three's is lighter, mirroring their physical differences.

One takes various items from the fridge and sets them out on the worktop, then reaches up to the top of the cupboard for the knife rack. That's not where it usually lives. They must've moved them up there when they arrived to avoid anyone having the chance to fight back.

It suddenly occurs to me that I've not seen a weapon on any of them, but they must have something somewhere. Why else would Grace and Jeremy be so afraid?

Needing to know exactly what I'm dealing with, I test the boundaries. "You're trusting me with a knife. Bit risky, don't you think?"

That seductive and dangerous smile spreads across One's face again. "Two, Three, what will you do if Rachel stabs me?" He finishes his question with a nod, gesturing for me to turn around.

Twisting cautiously, Two and Three wait for me to face them before they reach behind their backs and reveal their guns.

Say no more. No stabbing anyone today.

When I turn back to One, he's holding the knife out to me, handle first, but it's the other hand I focus on and the gun he cradles in it. Eyeing it cautiously, I take the knife from him before locking my gaze on his.

"Are you going to be a good girl?" he asks, and I nod in response.

Stepping up to the worktop, I grip the knife, taking a few calming breaths before chopping the onion in half. I may be cooler than Grace, but I'm also human—a mere mortal in a room with three armed men.

The acidic scent of the onion invades my nostrils, causing my eyes to sting, a shock to my senses that allows everything to sink in. This is the shit you see in movies, or occasionally on the news. The living nightmare that infiltrates the lives of a few unsuspecting people, but never us—until now.

This is real.

Before I have a chance to freak out, a warm, hard body presses against my back, and One's hands come into view. The first grips the wrist of the hand holding the knife, while the other slides over the one keeping the onion in place.

His breath tickles my cheek, sending electricity down my neck and straight to my core before his words fill my ear. "The thing is, though, Rachel," he whispers. "I'm not so sure you are a good girl."

One presses his groin into my lower back, and I inhale a shuddered breath. "I think you're a bad girl in good girls' clothing." He gently rolls his hips, and I squeeze my thighs together as my core throbs in response.

This is so wrong—my reaction, the location, the people in the room watching us—everything except his words.

"Can bad girls be good, Rach?" Fuck... the way he says it cuts deep, like an old wound ripping open. "Can you be a good girl for me?"

"One?" Two challenges, before the yes can fall past my lips. "Who said you get to have all the fun?"

In the blink of an eye, One spins me around to face the others, pointing my hand and the knife directly at them before stating, "I do."

Chapter Eight
Rachel

"Is there something wrong with your meal, Grace?" One asks, singling her out even though only he, his men, and the twins are eating. Jeremy, Grace, and I have moved the food around our plates, a forkful occasionally making its way into our mouths.

"Rachel worked hard on that," he adds, even though it's untrue. After squaring up to Two and Three courtesy of the knife in my hand, One stayed close, manoeuvring me around the kitchen as we cooked, his body an extension of mine. Now, he's next to me, with Grace and Jeremy on his left. Two and Three sit opposite us, and the twins sit on the side to my right, way too close to two loaded guns.

"Sorry, Rachel," Grace mumbles, forcing herself to chew a mouthful of spaghetti.

"Don't worry about it," I console, speaking directly to her for the first time this evening.

She smiles, only to jump out of her skin when Three drops his fork onto his empty plate and belches loudly, causing the twins to burst out laughing. Three smiles at them, like he's pleased with their approval, and I have to fight the sudden urge to launch my plate at him. My sisters don't see him as a threat, and I must keep them calm. One was right. If they freak out, tensions will rise, and I don't need anyone getting trigger-happy.

Clearing my throat, I get my sisters' attention. "Eat your dinner, you two." Smiling as I say it, they go back to their food, twisting the spaghetti around their forks. I wish I could be as oblivious as they are. I've had some awkward meals around this table, but this one takes the prize.

One's sigh brings my attention to him, and I notice he's also cleaned his plate. "Eat your dinner, Rachel," he says, using the same tone as I did when I spoke to the girls.

"I'm not hun—"

One's left hand slides up my dress, tightly gripping my thigh. Sensing my need to scream and fight him off, his eyes drift to my sisters, then back to me, a warning of what could happen if I make a scene.

Gritting my teeth, I bite out my words in a whisper. "Get. Off. Me."

"Eat," he orders.

"Get. Off!" I whisper more forcefully.

Shaking his head, he picks up my fork, gathers some food and lifts it to my mouth. "Eat, and I'll let go."

Fuck him and his ability to do whatever he wants—using my sisters against me—and fuck my body for wanting his hand to stay where it is, dangerously close to the ache his touch is creating.

Slowly, my eyes creep to the side, and I risk a glance at Grace and Jeremy—I don't know why; it's not like they'll save me.

True to form, they're both staring at their plates, ignoring the fact that I'm being groped by a masked armed man right in front of them.

What could they do anyway?

My gaze returns to One, and he squeezes my thigh, his thumb digging in hard enough to leave a mark. He doesn't blink, but his Adam's apple bobs, and his jaw tenses. The darker parts of me want to push him, to see how far he's prepared to go, but not here. Not now.

Breathing deeply, forcing my shaking thighs to remain still, I open my mouth to accept the food. His eyes fall to my lips, making me hyper-aware of every movement I make—my tongue reaching out, just a touch, my head pulling back as I clean the food off the fork, releasing it from my mouth.

One remains frozen in place, the fork in mid-air. Unable to break free from his gaze, I chew and swallow as quickly as possible, hoping it will break the spell and release the tension spreading throughout my body.

"Yummy," Two says, and, freeing me from One's mental hold, I turn to face him, dread replacing the tension when I realise his eyes are focused on my lap as *if he can see exactly what One is doing beneath my dress.*

This needs to stop. One may have this unexplainable power over me, but Two and Three don't, and the last thing I need is them thinking I'm open to offers.

Facing One again, I glare at him, rage and fear pulsing through my body. "I ate. Let go."

He doesn't move. Doesn't blink.

Leaning closer, I grit my teeth, keeping my voice low for the twins' sake. "I can't stop you being here, but you will keep your thieving hands off me."

One's mouth remains firm, but he closes the distance further, our faces barely an inch apart. "What if I ask nicely?" he whispers, but the sniggers from across the table suggest he wasn't quiet enough.

Holding my position, I keep my eyes on his. "The answer will be no."

"Oooh..."

One and I both face Three; he's staring at us, drumming his fingers across the table. "That's the problem with thieves, though, Rachel. They don't take no for an answer."

Chapter Nine
Nate

Alone in the kitchen, I slide my phone into my back pocket, step outside the back door and spark up a cigarette.

"Was that the boss?" Two asks. Loitering by the door, he nods towards me, so I reach into my pocket for my pack of Bensons, flipping the lid so he can grab one for himself.

Taking another deep inhale, I let him spark up before I reply. "He's just checking in." Making sure his daughter is alright. "Making sure we're all good with the new plan." The plan where I fuck his daughter so you can't.

"He worried?"

"He knows we can handle it." That part's true. The job isn't the issue here. Gesturing towards the house, I ask, "What's happening?"

"Three has settled the Grandparents in front of the TV, and our new friend is bathing the brats and getting them ready for bed."

Our... like fuck.

"She seems better at keeping her shit together than those two pretentious cunts. So, she has more than one purpose to serve while we're here."

Forcing a slow exhale, I try to remain calm—difficult since my body temperature is as hot as the ash falling from my cigarette. "Rachel's purpose... since she's here... will be to keep the children happy and out of our hair."

Two grins. "Right... and what was the purpose of you copping a feel?"

Mirroring his pose, I'm the epitome of nonchalance. "To ensure she understands the severity of the situation... she's not had as long to adapt."

Pursing his lips, Two nods in approval. "Glad we're on the same page. I'll be happy to help reinforce the message."

Breathe deep, Nathan. Breathe. Fucking. Deep.

"No. You won't." Inhaling the last of my cigarette, I stare him down, flicking my stub to the floor. "You and Three will be keeping your hands to yourselves. The job may have become more complicated than originally planned, but we can still do it clean." Pausing, I watch his reaction; the slight twitch of his jaw and sickening glint in his eyes show he's understood my meaning. Still, I make it crystal. "We don't need you making it messy."

Two moves further away from the house, joining me in the darkness. "I can handle my own, and I can handle her. She'll be as good as gold. No need to worry."

Clenching my fists so tight my knuckles crack, I grit out, "I'm not asking."

Two laughs, pulling his shoulders back to appear bigger. "I respect you, One—the boss too, but we know these fuckers won't talk, no matter what goes down in this house. We can get the job done and have some fu—"

My hand is around his throat before he can finish, and I have him pinned against the wall before he can gasp. "You. Will. Not. Touch. Rachel." Gripping his throat for another ten seconds, I release him and step back, giving him a chance to straighten himself out.

Many a man would lash out, but not Two. He lives for this shit, and he knows what would happen if he fucks with me.

Composing himself, he steps closer. "You're number one—I get that. But I agreed to what I agreed—Three did too—and little Rachel wasn't part of it." Seeing my fist clenched, Two raises a palm, appeasing me. "From what I've seen this evening, you're ready to play the man's game."

The man's game... This fool believes rape is a man's game. It takes all my strength not to crush his skull with my bare hands.

"You want her, you've made that clear, but Three and I are throwing our hats into the ring too, and we share," he adds, winking for effect. "You've not played with us before, but you know how it works." He tilts his head to the side, studying me. "You do know how it works, don't you?"

Oh, I know how it fucking works, and it's causing bile to creep up my throat. Forcing it down, my jaw aching as I grind out the words, "I don't share."

Snorting a laugh, Two steps back into the house. "Actions, One. You want her for yourself; it takes action. Words mean fuck all."

Chapter Ten
Rachel

"We don't want to play this game anymore," Bella whines as I tuck her and Ivy into their double bed. They've always shared a bed when they stay here, and tonight, I intend to be right in the middle of them, even if it means evicting their beloved collection of My Little Pony teddies.

Glancing at Ivy, I notice she's wearing the same worried expression as her sister. They're non-identical but so in tune. Ruffling their hair, I give a bright, fake smile. "What's the problem?"

Rising onto her elbows, Ivy takes over. "Well…" she huffs. "We don't like their masks, we don't like how sad Grandma looks, and we don't want to stay here all weekend."

"Why can't we go to yours?" Bella chimes in.

"Well..." Smirking at them, I mimic their expressions. "Grandma isn't sad; she's just tired from having you troublemakers all week." Pausing to tickle them, they give me a squeal in return. "And..." How the fuck do I play this? "Mummy and Daddy asked One, Two and Three to come and help... That's why they're here... To entertain us."

"Mummy and Daddy sent them?" they both chorus.

"Yes. They thought it would be fun, and they're paying them lots of money..." Or at least, they will. "Soooo... they can't leave until they come home."

Ivy flops back down dramatically, snuggling into her pillow. "They're scary," she whispers.

Climbing onto the bed, I wedge myself between them, wrapping an arm around each twin and pulling them close. "It's all just a game, remember? There's nothing to be scared of." Trying to take comfort in their silence, I do my best to convince myself my lies are true. It's impossible, though, because there are so many things to be afraid of: what will happen when Mum and Johnson get here, whether One will keep his word... and me. The way that part of all this feels so normal—the natural way of the world.

The strong defeat the weak, and the corrupt get their comeuppance.

Whether my reaction to One is my true self finally spilling over the walls of the prison I've kept her in all these years.

Shaking my head, I pull the twins closer, comforting myself more than them. "Anyway... what do you think I'd do if they were mean to you?" I challenge.

"Bite them!" Ivy announces triumphantly.

"Kick 'em in their peanuts!" Bella shouts, causing Ivy to burst out laughing.

"Cook them in a pie!" Ivy snorts.

"Yuck!" I laugh.

"Cut their guts out with a big knife, peel off their skin and then turn them into soup," Bella offers, silencing me.

Ivy and I share a look before turning over to face a grinning Bella. "Bella, sweetie..."

"Hmmm?"

"That was seriously... seriously dark."

What the hell do I do now?

The girls are finally asleep; it's eight o'clock, and I can still hear the TV, but I have no idea if I should stay here or join the others. I want to stay right here, curl up in bed where it's safe... away from temptation, but that makes me feel guilty for leaving Grace and Jeremy alone with the three psychos.

A gentle tapping at the door has me jumping to my feet, but before I can get there, it opens, revealing a silhouette of a man all in black. He looks like nothing more than a shadow. The room is dark, so the light behind him hides his features—the number on his hoodie. I don't need any of that, though. They each have a distinctive build, and if that wasn't enough, One's inviting scent and intoxicating energy will always give him away.

Putting the butterflies in my stomach, or in my case, moths, down to my fear of waking the girls, I walk straight towards him, causing him to step back, and pull the door closed behind me. "Please don't wake them. They're starting to get scared."

Nodding slowly, One grips my elbow and guides me across the hallway. Looking back at the closed door, wishing more than anything I could stand guard, I realise too late that I'm being led to a spare bedroom at the end of the landing.

My legs feel heavy, my stomach doing somersaults as One walks us into the room, flicks the switch, and then lightly closes the door. Feeling his presence behind me, I can only stare at the bed in front of me.

Do I turn and face him? Do I just stand and wait for the inevitable?

"Rachel..." he murmurs, and I slowly twist around until I face him. "We need to talk."

"I'd like to stay with the girls tonight," I blurt out in a panic. "I need them to be OK."

One steps closer, his hands so tight by his sides it's like he's forcing them to stay there. "Nothing is going to happen to them." He raises a finger to my face, holding it an inch from my lips when he sees I'm about to object. "But I understand, and that's fine."

Nodding my thanks, my eyes zone in on his finger, now moving towards my cheek, causing sparks to erupt from my skin when he connects, sweeping a few strands of hair behind my ear.

"You really weren't supposed to be here," he mumbles, more to himself than me. "It's a problem," he adds, his eyes landing on mine.

"I won't—"

"It's a problem for you," he warns, and it takes all my strength to stay standing. "Two and Three..." He pauses and releases a deep sigh, the lingering scent of tobacco on his breath, taking me back to the places I'd rather not venture.

I haven't smoked since I left London. Like the memories, the nicotine was too painful to swallow.

Oblivious to the trauma he's inflicting on me, One's eyes dart to the floor. "They aren't... they have certain expectations..." His Adam's apple bobs as he forces a swallow before staring right at me. "There are things that society condemns that they think are normal."

Taking a deep breath in, I attempt to make my voice work. One seems to think that keeping us all hostage and robbing us is acceptable. I don't know where he draws the line, but I must. "Like what?"

"Rape." He says it so calmly, but the word has me staggering back until I bump into the last place I need to be. Falling backwards onto the bed, I try to scramble away, but One pins me in place, his legs on either side of mine, and he seals my mouth closed with his large hand.

"No screaming… OK? Remember those sisters of yours." He looks me dead in the eyes, knowing that's all he needs to say to make me hold it together.

Swallowing the rising bile, I nod, but he keeps his hand where it is. "Two and Three might be animals, but they have some rules. I can keep them away from you. Do you want that?"

Nodding frantically, I lift my hand and shove his away from my mouth. "Please…" I beg.

"They'd hurt you," he continues as if I haven't spoken, and as my heart fills with dread, tears fall down my cheeks. I hate crying in front of people, but I leave the tears where they are, hoping to appeal to his humanity.

Lowering his face towards mine, One's mouth rests against my ear. "You have a choice to make, Rachel."

My next breath catches in my throat because I know I won't like it.

"You can come for me or bleed for them."

Blackness swallows me whole as I feel myself sinking into the mattress. Blood rushes to my brain, almost sending me blind with dizziness. One grips my shoulders, shaking me, pulling me back, and I gasp for air, trying to get enough clarity to force him away.

That's my choice... deciding who gets to rape me? Choosing between one man or two. It doesn't matter what he made me feel earlier. All I can think of is fighting. He wants to take away the one thing I've always battled to retain: the power to decide what happens to my body.

"Get off!" *I shout, and One's hand silences me again.*

"It's the only way, Rachel. I'll treat you good, but they'll take pleasure in breaking you."

Kicking against his hold causes him to use more strength, and it only takes a few seconds to restrict my movement completely.

"Listen to me," *he pleads against my ear.* "This is happening. One way or another... me or them, but it's happening." *Nestling his nose in my hair, he inhales deeply as if trying to calm his raging heart.* "What if I told you we've done this before?"

Everything stops. No sounds. No air in my lungs, only One's voice ringing through my head.

Lifting his body a few inches away, One removes his hand from my mouth, and I inhale as much air as possible. Staring at him, I try to see beyond the mask, but it covers too much.

"Liar," *I choke, and he shakes his head in response.*

Caressing my bottom lip with his thumb, he gently pulls it down. "I've kissed you here before." *He's so confident it leaves no room for doubt.*

One sits taller, his weight keeping my hips in place, not that I'm fighting him now—I'm too shocked to do anything. I thought he was familiar the second I met him, but this… I never expected this. Wracking my brain, I stare into those eyes while his hands slide down my body. Every time I've had sex, I've done so with a clear head. I knew exactly what I was doing, but the truth is, not everyone was memorable.

He could be anyone.

Pausing at my left breast, he gently cups it. "I've sucked on this nipple." Moving over to my other breast, he squeezes it with a smirk. "This one, too."

Sparks shoot through my body as his words and touch ignite something deep within. A memory of what once was or a brand-new desire, I don't know, but either way, I shouldn't be feeling it.

Leaning lower, One's masked face hovers over mine. "Not ringing any bells?" Humming, he nips my neck, and I arch my back in response.

No, no, no…It shouldn't feel this good.

"How many men have you had, Rachel?" It's an accusation, and the mist lifts and a new heat rushes at me.

"That's none of your fucking business!" I snap. A man forcing himself on me has no right to ask that— no one does.

"Isn't it?" Switching his weight to his left elbow, he toys with my hair with one hand whilst stroking my cheek with the other. "Did it help?"

My mouth flies open, but no words come out. I don't know if I'm more scared, angry or confused, but all three emotions are more palatable than being aroused.

Locking his eyes on mine, One looks right through me as if he already knows the answers to the questions I've no idea how to contemplate. "Did it solve all your problems?"

Slam! His hand covers my mouth before he's finished speaking, preventing the scream I'm ready to unleash.

My heart goes back to hammering against my chest as something too close to realisation floods my senses.

Did it solve my problems?

What? The men? The sex?

Why would he ask that specific question?

Those are my words, spoken years ago and only ever to one person. That night. The last night I remember being truly happy. When more than one secret was promised to the shadows forever.

It can't be.

Struggling against his weight does nothing to shift him, so I sink my teeth into his palm. "Fuck!" he yells, snatching it away.

Pulling his sleeve over his hand, he smothers my mouth before I can produce a sound.

"Rach..." It's a whispered plea that barely registers. All I can think of is freeing my hands so I can rip off his mask. See with my eyes what my heart already knows is true.

Knock. Knock. Knock.

That—I hear. Three knocks that cause us both to freeze. Our hearts beat at the same, frantic rhythm, the sound practically echoing around the room, but not loud enough to stop the next noise from reaching my ears—the light screech of the door handle twisting.

I focus only on One, the plea now in my eyes. I didn't make my choice, but if this is my chance, then he needs to know I choose him.

"Open up," a voice calls. I can't tell who it is, and I don't care. One locked the door. That's all that matters right now.

Staring at him, I force my limbs to relax and shake my head, hoping he can interpret my silent message.

"Sounds like you need a hand," the voice mocks, and I shake my head again.

One presses a finger to his lips in warning, and as I nod, he pulls his hand away.

Inhaling a deep breath, I whisper, "Please don't let him in."

Watching me for a moment, One licks his lips. "You need to say it."

Tears burn my eyes, but I refuse to let them fall. I don't even know why they're here... anger, despair, heartbreak, or complete and utter relief. Whatever the reason, I can't comprehend it right now. I have a sliver of control, a way to limit the damage, and I will take it.

Swallowing hard, I nod my head, staring One in the eyes. "Just you," I croak out. "Please... just you."

One's shoulders rise like a weight's been lifted off them, and he turns towards the door. "I already told you. I. Don't. Share."

The laugh that snakes through the cracks in the door makes my skin crawl. The threat is as evident as *if he were in this room with us. "Better get it done, then."*

One remains focused on the door until we hear the footsteps descending the stairs, and then he turns to me. It's just the two of us in this room. There are six more people in this house, but they may as well not exist.

My focus darts between his eyes and his lips, and I let the image of the boy from my memories, sitting above me just like One is, back into my mind. I kicked him out years ago, but I need him now. I need to know that he and what I thought he once felt are now in this room.

Swallowing, I moisten my dry throat. "No," I whisper. Pausing, I take a few deep breaths, trying to lessen the pain in my chest. "Sex doesn't solve anything."

One shakes his head. "Today... it does." Lowering his body, he places a hand on each side of my head, the mattress dipping with his weight. "Today..." He pauses and clears his throat. "I won't let you fall, Rachel."

Sirens blare in the distance, the night breeze chills my skin, nicotine coats my tongue, and I take a leap, but only in my head. Squeezing my eyes tightly shut only causes the tears to spill over, so I force them open, my blurry gaze landing on the mask that denies me the truth... and a possible way out of this. "Show me," I demand. "Prove it."

One's warm breath fans my face as he exhales. "Only if you make me a promise." He doesn't wait for my response. "If you promise that the only name that leaves your lips when I make you come is One."

Chapter Eleven
Nate

Rachel's eyes darken, and she remains frozen, but she's smart. She'll understand. "Take off the mask," *she demands.*

"Promise."

"You'll always be just One." *Her words sting way more than they should.* "And you have no chance of making me come."

Did then. Will now.

Knowing that a smile will piss her off even more, I keep my face void of emotion as I take to me feet and slowly pull off the mask. The relief is instant, my skin tingling when it makes contact with the warm air, but my gaze remains on Rachel—the recognition in her eyes and the shape her mouth is making.

"Na—"

I'm on her in a second, my hand clamping her mouth shut for about the tenth time since this shitshow started. "One," I grit out. "That's the only name you know, understand?"

The fire in her eyes shows she's not done fighting, but she nods, agreeing to my terms, so I slowly remove my hand and lean back.

Rachel slides off the bed and stands before me. Staring at me, she studies every inch of my face. If she likes what she sees, she's certainly not showing it. I want her to. I want that yearning, that fucking love she once gave me back.

"Is he behind this?"

He… Tony—her dad.

If anyone else asked me this question, I'd cut out my tongue before telling the truth, but we're on this path now. I chose honesty to make it easier for her— no. Not true. I let her know who I am because I want her to want it—to want me.

Deciding silence is the safest bet, I nod.

Fisting her hands, she raises them and presses them against her forehead. "You fucking cunts," she grinds out.

"Quiet," I warn.

"How could he do this to me?"

"You weren't supposed to be—"

She shoves me in the chest before I can finish, but I grab hold of both her wrists and push her against the nearest wall, easily keeping her at bay. Rachel barely notices, too focused on what she has to say. "My sisters are… my mum will be. For fuck's sake! My mum. My fucking mum. He was married to her!" She's furious, but keeping her voice low, so I let her spit her venom. She's entitled. "Is this payback?"

Not against you. "It's a pay cheque."

"He's the one going to pay!" Her voice rises, and I smother her with my body.

"Do I have to give this mouth something else to do? They. Can't. Hear. This." I nod towards the door, ensuring she understands.

Laughing bitterly, she tries to free her wrists, failing. "They can't touch me. Neither can you."

"They don't know who you are."

"Then tell them!" she demands. "They're working for my dad. If he cares anything for me at all, then he would kill them first."

"Rach—"

"And you..." She gets right in my face, thankfully keeping her voice low enough that it won't travel beyond this room. "It's me or them... Like fuck! You can't—"

Slamming my mouth against hers seems like a good idea since my hands are still gripping her wrists, but after about two seconds, her shock fades, and her teeth sink into my bottom lip.

It feels way too good.

Groaning at the contact, the heat, and the pain, I yank her from the wall, push her onto the bed and jump straight on top of her, using my large hand to silence her—again.

"Time to listen," I grit the words out with a pant, the adrenaline, fear of being caught, and arousal from being so close to her body making me breathless. "I didn't lie to you."

She wriggles against me, her insults dying in the flat of my palm.

"If they find out who you are, they'll know we lied to them. Your dad lied to them. This was supposed to be clean—no ties, no comeback." I stare her down, ensuring she can see how serious I am. "Telling them who you are won't keep them from you... It would be a death sentence for everyone in this house."

Rachel stills, my words sinking in, and I take the chance and remove my hand from her mouth. "I swear... this was supposed to be over with by now—no harm done, but we're too close to walk away, and I promise you..." Pausing, I inhale another deep breath. "If I don't have you, they will... your dad knows this, too."

Choking on her bitter laugh, she shakes her head. "My dad told you to rape me?"

"No... I would nev—" Gripping the sheets, I crush them between my fingers and lower my head to hers. "I told you all this to make it easier... So you wouldn't be afraid."

Silence fills the room; my heart beats against my chest, but Rachel lies there frozen.

Looking beyond me, she stares at the wall for what feels like a lifetime. The lifetime I lived without her. "But it has to happen." Her eyes narrow, her jaw tenses, and her hate-filled gaze lands on me. "Let's get it over with then."

Wriggling away, Rachel climbs off the bed, shooting daggers at me as she hastily pulls down her tights and throws them to the floor. Next, she reaches for the hem of her figure-hugging dress, yanks it over her head, and then launches it at mine. She's practically steaming with rage, and in any other situation, I'd laugh at her dramatics. Not today, and I make no attempt to catch the dress, too mesmerised by the body she's exposing.

Jesus. Fucking. Christ.

The last time I saw her like this, we were practically children. Rachel was beautiful, her delicate curves starting to show. Now, she's all woman with a body to kill for... and kill me she could, if the look in her eyes is anything to go by.

Without hesitation, she reaches behind her back with both hands, releasing the clasp on her bra, the black lace slapping my cheek when it hits me. Death by underwear... There are worse ways to go.

Rachel isn't trying to be sexy. She's not putting on a show. She's livid, and when she slides down her underwear, she stalks back to the bed and spreads her legs, revealing her sweet cunt to me, then beckons me to join her with a dismissive flick of her wrists. "I hope you still have my condoms," she deadpans. "Who knows where you've been."

Chapter Twelve
Nate

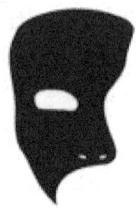

"Quick, quick." Rachel snaps her fingers when I don't move.

Funny. Everything about her is hilarious. She thinks this will be just business—that we're simply proving to Two and Three that the deed was done. Quick, this will not be. I've been denied this for years; tonight, I'll take my sweet time.

Giving her an appraising smile that barely reveals a hint of my admiration, I pull the gun from where it rests against my back, place it on the nearby shelf, unzip my hoodie, and let it drop to the floor. "You grew up." My eyes travel across her body, landing again on the sweet cunt I claimed first and will reclaim tonight.

"Tends to happen." Rachel tries to seem unbothered, but a flash of red creeps across her chest when I remove my t-shirt, revealing a body sculpted in the streets—by surviving, not hitting the gym.

Trying my best not to preen as her eyes rake over my body, I kick off my shoes, remove my socks and pull my tracksuit bottoms and boxers down in one fell swoop. My cock springs free, and when Rachel gasps, I lock my eyes on hers and give it a few pumps, tightly squeezing my shaft.

Squirming, she focuses on my eyes, rights herself, and then tips her head towards my throbbing erection. "I guess you grew up, too."

Yes. I did.

Stalking over to her, her false confidence falters, and when she starts to close her legs, I quickly fill the space, keeping her nice and wide for me. "Where do you think you're going?"

Rachel's pupils dilate, and her chest heaves, but that stubborn chin juts out. "You forgot the condom."

A lazy smile stretches across my face as I grip her right knee with one hand and gently slide the other up her leg. Relishing in her softness, her warmth, my cock twitching when her legs jerk in response. "Patience."

Grabbing my roaming hand, she squeezes it tightly. "All you need to do is make the headboard bash against the wall a few times and fill the condom. That's all the proof they need."

"You got bossy, too," I chuckle. "Actually, no. You were always a demanding little brat." I wince when she twists my wrist. "See me." I mock. "Want me…" Her nails dig in. "Touch me."

"I was fiftee—"

"I did all those things, Rachel." I ignore her protests. "I saw, I wanted, and I touched." Staring her in the eyes, I ignore the pain she's inflicting, focusing instead on her scent, her growing arousal. "It was wrong then... hmmm... so some would say... and it may be wrong now. But guess what."

"What?" she grits out.

Moving in on her causes her to pull away, but the only place she has to go is back—on her back—exactly where I want her. "You loved it then, and you'll love it now."

"Just get it over with," she begs in a whisper before remembering who the fuck she is. "I barely remember it, so there's no need for a trip down memory lane."

Now pinning her to the bed with my body, I yank my wrist from her grip, giving it a gentle twist to ease the ache. She drew blood. Good. It'll look like she put up a fight.

Nuzzling into her neck, I whisper, "You remember my birthday, though... don't you?" She flinches, and I lean back so I can watch her reaction. It doesn't disappoint. Rachel's face burns brightly, her eyebrows shooting to the ceiling. She didn't know who I was when she gave me the code to her phone. When she said the last number, my heart nearly burst out of my chest and hit the wall. My birthday. After all these years, my birthday is the passcode to her phone. It was almost enough to make me forget about the condoms she carries with her.

"I've used the same number for years." Rachel's jaw is rigid, her eyes frozen wide, forcing herself not to blink. "It means nothing other than I was too lazy to change it."

Who's she trying to convince? Keen to see how long she can maintain the pretence, I refuse to look away. "Still such a little liar," I whisper.

Escape is futile, but she still tries, so I grab both her wrists and yank them over her head, then secure them in place in one hand. Rachel's as tough as they come, always has been, but I'm stronger.

"Fuck. You," she grinds out. "I never lied to you. You were the liar."

The words slice us both, her vulnerability shining in her eyes. She has every right to be angry with me, but we can rake over the past later. "As much as I love this chat," I deadpan. "I'd rather make you come before Two and Three kick the door down." That gets her attention, and she flinches at the thought. "You're soaking wet, and they can probably smell you from downstairs."

Rachel's face flushes red, but before she can rage at me, I slide two fingers inside her cunt. Pushing them deep, giving her no time to adjust and showing her no mercy, I press my thumb against her clit. Her scream of shock is exquisite and serves a purpose for those listening below.

Rachel's eyes lock on mine, her gaze a mixture of surprise, hate and lust.

"Try not to come too loudly, Rachel." Staring her down, I start to pump my fingers in and out, circling her clit with my thumb at the same time, adding just the right amount of pressure to ease her in. "Your pleasure is just for me. Another secret."

Rachel's eyes start to roll back, but she blinks, trying not to give in to the inevitable. She's only making it worse for herself. Adding more pressure, I pump harder, and a moan escapes her mouth before she sinks her teeth into her bottom lip, forcing them closed.

"You are going to come for me, Rachel. The only thing up for debate is how many times." Pumping faster, I add a third finger. Rachel's mouth remains firmly closed, but she arches her back and strains her neck, forcing her head into the pillow.

"And where..." I continue as I spit against her clit, mixing it with her juices, as my thumb works her even harder. As silent as she's staying, her walls grip my fingers, and her knees shake. She can't hide it. "I want you to come all over my fingers, in my mouth and on my dick."

Rachel's eyes snap open, her lips part, and she inhales deeply, but instead of revealing her pleasure, she unleashes more hate. "You don't have it in you."

Letting go of her wrists, I reach forward and grab her chin, holding her in place as I steal her mouth. She resists, but I nip her lips, forcing my way in until my tongue dances with hers.

"Come on my hand. Now," I order, pumping even harder than before. Rachel's got some serious willpower, but my hand will fall off before I give in. Her body is ready to go; it's only her head keeping her from tipping over the edge.

"No."

So. Fucking. Stubborn.

"No?" I hum before sucking her bottom lip into my mouth and holding it between my teeth. Rachel gasps, and I release her lip with a pop before moving down her body. Wasting no time, I clamp my teeth around her left nipple and bite down. I feel her release coming before I hear the moan escaping, and as Rachel's body shakes beneath me, she presses both hands firmly against her mouth, muffling her screams.

Precum leaks from the tip of my cock, but I'm not finished with her yet. Rachel set me a challenge, and she's going to fucking lose. She's still moaning and writhing against my soaked hand, but I release her nipple.

"Look at me," I order, breathless and husky.

Rachel peels her eyes open, barely able to focus.

"You should pick your battles better." Sliding down her body, I withdraw my fingers using both hands to force her legs even wider before diving face-first into her cum-soaked core. I'm so desperate to taste her again that I shove my tongue inside, fucking her and swallowing all she has.

"N... no... no more," she forces out through her gasps, but all it does is fuel me on because Two and Three need to hear her objecting.

As for me, I'm not sure I could stop even if I thought she meant it. Rachel agreed we needed to do this, but she thought it would be a simple transaction—that she'd call the shots. I'm making her mine, and she can't stand giving in, no matter how much she loves the warmth and pleasure shooting through her body.

Pulling my tongue out, I slide up, sucking her clit into my mouth. She's still riding the waves of her first orgasm, and I refuse to let her rest. I lick, nip, suck with all I have, almost dizzy with the speed of my movements. Rachel starts grinding against my face, and one of her hands grips my head, nails digging into my scalp, keeping me exactly where I am.

Spurred on by her need, I push two fingers back inside. They know exactly where to go, and within seconds, Rachel is squirting.

This time, she can't stop the moan from escaping, her pleasure free for all to hear, and I'm too lost in her to consider stopping her. Resting my mouth against her entrance, I coat my tongue in her cum, groaning in pleasure while I grind my throbbing erection into the mattress.

I need her. Now.

Jumping off the bed, I grab the pack of condoms from my hoodie, rip one open and slide it over my dick. I'm back on the bed in the blink of an eye. Rachel is gasping for air, her hands gripping her thighs, but I rip them away and hover above her. Her eyes land on mine when she feels my tip at her entrance. Her despair is amusing—so conflicted between hating and loving what I'm doing to her.

"Two down," I state, barely holding it together. "If you can't keep that lying mouth shut when you come on my dick, what name are you going to call?"

An inaudible sound leaves her mouth, but her eyes tell me she is planning to object, so I force my dick inside.

"Fuuuck...." I groan at the same time as Rachel mumbles incoherently. It takes a few seconds for me to ground myself and get my head in the game because she feels so good. Sliding a hand around her throat, I pull her attention from the ceiling back to me.

"I asked..." Thrust. "When you come on my dick." Thrust and a mutual groan of appreciation. "What. Name. Are. You. Going. To. Call?" I punctuate each word by slamming into her, my balls bouncing against her arse, the slapping of flesh against flesh filling my ears, forcing me to grip my shaft before I end this whole thing now.

"One," Rachel whispers hoarsely.

Squeezing her neck more tightly, I start to pump my hips in an even rhythm as I lower my head so I can whisper in her ear. "I didn't hear you."

"One," she calls on a gasp, the word flying from her mouth involuntarily.

"That's right." Releasing her neck, I find her lips; this time, she initiates the kiss. Her tongue searches for mine, and I give it to her willingly.

This isn't going to last long.

Our sweat-slicked bodies slide against each other as we move in a blissful, punishing rhythm. She meets each of my thrusts with her own, causing the headboard to slam against the wall, announcing to everyone that I'm making her mine.

"One… I was the first one…" I pant, gripping her cheeks so her eyes stay on mine. They're slipping to the back of her head, but she's trying to focus. "I should've been the only one."

The confession falls past my lips with the realisation that it's my fault—that I was the one who set her free for others to taste, and it has me thrusting into her at a punishing speed. Rachel's nails dig into my shoulders, and her core spasms against my dick. Her mouth starts to open, and this time, I want to keep her pleasure just for me. Slamming my lips against hers, I swallow her moans, only letting myself go when her body stops shaking.

Chapter Thirteen
Nate

She's been in the ensuite long enough.

Pushing myself up from the bed, I stride towards the locked door. Giving two sharp knocks, I rest my forehead against the cool wood. "Open up." No answer. "You can't stay in there all night. Who will watch over your sisters?"

The latch turns immediately like I knew it would. Opening the door, I step in cautiously, trusting my instincts—quite rightly. The second my whole body is in the bathroom, a fist flies into my stomach as a towel-clad Rachel attempts to silently unleash her fury on me.

She got lucky, but I was expecting something, so it only takes a moment to recover. Grabbing her wrists, I yank them behind her back and pull her body flush *against mine. It was a bad idea not to put some clothes on before I came in here. Not only did I leave my dick vulnerable to her wrath, I have no way of hiding what being this close to her does to me.*

"You. Fucking. Bastard," she grinds out in a whisper.

At least she understands the need to keep quiet.

"I always knew that you didn't give a shit, but I thought deep down my dad might care. What a stupid bitch I was."

Wrong on both counts.

"How—"

My hand slamming over her mouth cuts her off, and I take a chance and release her wrists. "Shut. Up."

Rachel's chest heaves and her eyes widen, the warrior inside—her father's daughter—clawing at the seams of her practised reserve. Rachel was always explosive.

"I told you already. You weren't supposed to be here."

Ripping my hand from her mouth, Rachel's jaw clenches as she fights to keep her voice low. "My little sisters are, and they don't deserve this. They're not part of this world."

"So, it's a good job they think it's all a game."

Stepping back, Rachel pulls her towel tighter. My naked body instantly misses her warmth. "Yeah... Sure, Nate. Just one big game where you get to fuck me with my waste of space of a dad's permission. And to think we were so worried all those years ago." Rachel scoffs as her eyes roam over me, repulsed. "It has to be our secret, Rach. He can never know," she mocks, repeating my words from the first time I touched her.

"Are you done being a cunt?"

Rachel flies at me, fist at the ready, but I catch her, shoving her back hard into the wall.

"If you want to bring up the past, then let's at least do it truthfully," I grit out, my anger bubbling to the surface. "Because your version is bullshit."

Eight Years Ago

Monday

Staring at the last message Rachel sent me, like a pussy-whipped cunt, I sit on my bed, delaying the one thing I'm supposed to be doing—replying to Tony. He's lined me up for a job tonight, and I want it. I need it since the electric meter ran out this morning, but I can't get my head in the game.

I crossed a line on Thursday night. It was inevitable, let's face it, but I'm now seriously fucked. Or I will be. I'm shitting my pants, waiting for Rachel to get home so we can figure this out together. I can't believe her mum let her skip school, but I heard them fighting on Friday morning. Trish knew something happened, so I assume it's an attempt to keep Rachel from me.

Not gonna happen.

Trish has had her weekend to, hopefully, calm down, but this is where their life is. She's got to come back soon. When she does... well. Rachel does what she wants, and she wants me. The only way her mum can keep us apart is if she chooses to land me in it with Tony. She's not done it yet because he'd have been over already, but it doesn't mean she won't. Trish can be a vindictive bitch when she wants to be, but Tony still loves her, and, whatever he thinks of me, he loves his daughter even more.

Tuesday

Rubbing my eyes, I wake up from my restless sleep, phantom banging plaguing my mind. After finally returning Tony's call, I went to work collecting a debt from some git who nearly stabbed me—very nearly— then came home. It's the closest I've ever come to getting seriously hurt, and I keep playing the beating that I dished out after I managed to dodge the blade, every time I close my eyes. Broken teeth have a way of doing that.

It's not the first time I've had to remind people what it means to cross Tony, but it's the first time I've hurt someone out of pure hate. The debt didn't call the damage I inflicted, the blood spilt… but he almost had me, and it made me feel weak. I didn't like that. My dad made me weak—until he couldn't—but nobody else ever will.

After cleaning off in the shower, I called Rach and found peace. She has no idea, but she's my sanctuary. She's pulled me back from the edge more times than she'll ever know. It's been torture being apart from her, but she's coming home today, and I need to figure out what we do next. Staying away isn't an option, even if it were geographically possible; we don't want to be apart. Rach has made that clear, and so have I.

Rolling out of bed for a piss, another bang gets my attention. It wasn't a dream; it was coming from Rachel's flat this whole time.

Checking my phone, I take in the time—2 pm—that's what happens when you're too cold to sleep at night. No longer feeling the need to relieve my bladder, I grab the nearest clothes and race out of my flat. A waft of stale cigarettes invades my nostrils as I pull my hoodie over my head, but washing can wait.

"Whatcha."

"Sorry, mate," *I say on instinct as my head clears the gap and my surroundings come into view. I'd nearly crashed into an old chap, arms wrapped around a box… leaving Rachel's flat.*

Taking a moment to process what I'm seeing, I step back and laugh. "Old man," *I tut.* "I hope you know whose flat you're stealing from." Tony doesn't technically own it, but his claim over the people here remains.

Clearing his throat, the man slowly lowers the box to the floor and, to my surprise, smiles and extends his hand. "Dennis."

Dennis... I know that name. Shit. "As in, Grandad Dennis?"

"Dad?"

Both Dennis and I turn when Trish calls from the doorway. Her dark hair is scraped back from her flushed cheeks, and the look in her eyes when they land on me screams bloody murder.

"Can you manage this one, too?"

Dennis picks up the box he'd been carrying and braces himself for the extra weight as Trish adds another.

"This him?" Dennis gestures towards me, the soft look in his eyes from before now gone. All Trish does is nod in return before walking straight back into the flat.

Dennis says nothing more as he makes his way to the lift, and I rush straight in behind Trish, heading for Rachel's room. Empty. It is not just missing Rachel; all her things are gone or in boxes.

Heat races through my body, my chest constricting, as I turn, unbalanced, and march back into the living room. "What the fuck?"

Throwing whatever she was holding to the floor, Trish rushes at me. "Don't you talk to me like that! Don't you ever fucking talk to me like that."

Gritting my teeth, I use my height to my advantage and tower over her. "What. The. Fuck. Are. You. Doing?"

Snorting a laugh, she shakes her head at me, reminding me that Tony's ex isn't intimidated by a kid like me. "I'm taking my daughter far away from here."

"You're leaving?" The words stumble out, all my bravado gone as my grip on reality wavers. "Does Tony—"

"Not yet," she answers, knowing what I'm going to ask. "But he will. When I'm ready."

"You're not taking Rachel anywhere. He won't allow it." Adrenaline pumps through me, causing my fingers to shake, and I reach into my pocket, only to remember my phone is back at mine.

Trish hands me hers, a knowing smile on her face. "Call him," she challenges. "Who do you think he'll be angrier with? Me... or you?"

There's no doubt she'll tell him here and now that I spent the night with Rachel. That his precious, underage daughter is no longer a virgin because of me.

"Or... we could chat, Nate." She looks at me like she once did. The poor boy from next door whose mum's always passed out and his dad used to knock seven shades of shit out of him. "We could have a real, honest chat about doing the right thing for someone we both love."

Chapter Fourteen
Rachel

Breathing deeply, I keep my eyes closed, not wanting to look at Nate. His face, his body, his fucking presence is too distracting, and I'm trying my best to focus on what he just told me. To blend his story with my version of events.

It's not true.

"I called you. Every day..." My eyes open of their own accord, and I stare him down. "For weeks," I grit out. "I got nothing from you."

Nate swallows hard, his Adam's apple bobbing. "I know."

"My heart was fucking breaking!" Gasping, as if I can feel it still, that raw punch in the gut, my heart bruised and aching. "I needed... I needed you to talk to me."

"I... I agreed to let you go."

"To save your skin, right? To stop her from telling my dad."

"No..." he shakes his head, and if I were still fifteen, I might believe he cared. "I couldn't give you the life you deserved, Rach. Trish made me see that."

Needing an outlet for the unwelcome pain, I shove him away. "You should've talked to me, Nate!" My voice rises on his name, and he slams his hand over my mouth with such force that my head jerks back against the wall.

I don't care.

Shoving his hand away, my anger matching his, I keep my voice low. "You were right. My life was a million times better without you in it." The lie tastes bitter because it's pathetic—the fact that my statement isn't true is utterly pitiful. "I have good friends. A great job."

That part is true. Still, it's never been enough, which stings, so I take it out on Nate. "If I'd stayed in London... with you... I'd be passed out on the sofa like your mum every night, trying to drown my miserable fucking existence with a bottle of cheap vodka."

Nate smiles, sending chills down my spine. It's the smile of a man on the edge of an explosion. It reaches his eyes and fills them with malice. I'm so lost in them that I don't realise his right hand creeps towards my neck until he wraps it tightly around my skin.

"Wrong again, Rach." Leaning lower, his nose touches mine, such a gentle action and a stark contrast to the hand at my throat. "There would've been shit to deal with, things I needed to keep you away from, but if you'd have stayed with me, you'd have known how it felt to be cherished. To never want for anything because I'd know what you needed before you realised it yourself. If you were too hot, I'd make hell freeze over to cool you down, and I'd burn the entire world if I saw you so much as shiver."

Using his free hand, Nate's fingertips snake up my arm, leaving an eruption of goosebumps and electricity in his wake. "Our life would've been chaotic, messy and unpredictable." Moving towards my ear, my shallow breaths catch as I gasp for them; Nate whispers, "It would've been perfect."

Attempting to regain control, I force his hand away. "Anyone would think you regretted your choice," I bite out. "Not me. I don't like chaos. I like the way things are."

Nate's low chuckle vibrates through my entire body, setting off an ache in my core. "More lies." Studying my face for what feels like forever while I do my best to maintain my pretence, Nate finally speaks. "You're dead on the inside."

"Fu—"

Nate's lips stop my protests, his tongue forcing its way into my mouth as his hands pull the towel wrapped around me away from my body. I have no idea where it lands because I'm too busy pulling his chest against mine, bringing him back to me, waking myself up.

He's right, and we both know it, but it's a sad reality I don't want to admit. Instead, I put everything into the kiss, our tongues clashing as we nip, lick and suck in a desperate attempt to take what we both need.

Nate's hands pinch my butt cheeks as he lifts me, pressing his dick against my soaked core. Grabbing a fistful of my hair, he pulls my head back. "Have you ever been fucked bare?" he demands.

"N-no. Agh!"

Nate slams inside me, pressing his body against me as he fills me. "The first one," he smiles. "Again." Pulling back, leaving just the tip, he thrusts back into me, the force knocking the air from my lungs. "The. Only. One." Nate punctuates each word by slamming his hips against me, the onslaught leaving me breathless, relying on his strength to keep me upright.

Nate keeps up his pace and brutality like a man possessed, forcing weak cries from my throat. He releases a guttural groan, not caring who may hear, while my grip on reality slips. Everything he's said and done screams that I matter, but the crushing burden of grief that I carry from all those years ago keeps those hopes at bay.

Hope has no place here. There's only regret, betrayal, and the desperate need to heal our wounds. My nails dig into Nate's shoulders as he drives deeper, taking me closer to an earth-shattering orgasm. My body starts to shake, and Nate's fingers dig into my chin, tilting my eyes towards his.

"One," he gasps on a moan—a reminder to keep my head and remember the consequences of revealing our secret.

"I hate you," I murmur in response as I feel myself tipping over the edge.

Nate follows right after me, sucking at the sensitive skin on my neck, muffling his moans as his body shudders. He stays there for a minute, keeping me close as he catches his breath.

Lifting his head, our sweat-slicked foreheads meet, our breath mingling as we fight to fill our lungs with air. "Hate never felt so good," he whispers. "And regret never looked so beautiful."

Chapter Fifteen
Nate

Treating her like the queen she is, I guide Rachel's legs back to the floor and pull out. She wobbles, so I hold her close and walk her towards the sink. Keeping my arm wrapped around her waist, I pick up a flannel from the stack on display and run it under the warm tap.

Rachel is finally silent, the fight on hold while she regains her strength. Her eyes snap to mine when she feels the warmth against her thighs, but she's locked herself away. Unreachable again.

Looking down, feeling only pride when I see my cum smeared on the pale blue cotton—a question hitting me a little too late. "I realise I should've asked this before, but... are you on the pill?"

Her deep exhale is silent, but the force of it reaches my skin in a flash of heat. "Bit late. But yes, I am."

Tilting her head to the side, a spark returns to her eyes. "Is there anything I should be concerned about?"

"Plenty," I retort, "but not what you're suggesting." Satisfied she's clean, I pass her a new towel.

"What now?" she asks, her voice weary.

"Now, you try and get some sleep." Guiding her away from the wall, quietly enjoying that she isn't fighting me, I lead her back into the bedroom.

Rachel gathers her clothing from where she flung it, redressing far slower than she stripped them off. This room feels like a temporary haven—to me, at least—I'm in no rush to leave it.

Dressed in everything but my mask, I lead her to the door. "Wait."

She pauses, her shoulders low, defeated, and turns.

"Tomorrow is going to be a long day. I need to know you can keep it together."

Rachel stares at the wall behind me, a slight tip of her head showing her consent.

It's not enough. Gripping her chin, I force her to face me. "I mean it." Rachel remains silent, her eyes locked on mine. "I'm One. Never Nate. I'm not someone you care about."

"I don't," she snaps.

Ignoring her, I push on. "We both have a part to play… especially me. Remember that."

Rachel has questions brimming, but there's no time. Replacing my mask, I guide her from the room back to where the girls are. Handing her the key, which *she immediately snatches, I give her a final warning. "Only open this door for me."*

She greets me with more silence, which is for the best, and I wait until I hear the door is locked and she's safe behind it before walking down the stairs to where Two and Three wait. We agreed masks will always stay on, even when we're alone. There's always a chance of a hidden camera somewhere.

Following the smell of their cigarettes, I enter the kitchen, finding both men leaning back with their feet on the table. Three spots me first, a devilish smile that reveals crooked teeth and a stained soul spreads across his face, and he slaps his hands together in a loud clap.

"Good lad," Three announces. "Didn't think you had it in you but fuck me, can the slag still walk?"

Slag. Thank fuck for the mask, hiding what that word does to me. That's what they think of women— they're just there to use and abuse, and they make it their fault afterwards.

"Just about," I laugh, a hollow sound lost in their jeers. Rubbing my wrist, I make sure they see the scratches—that she put up a fight.

"Got to say, though, One," Two joins in. "There were some unusual sounds coming from that room."

"Is that so?" Sitting at the table, I keep myself distracted—appearing unbothered—by grabbing a cigarette from the open pack in front of me. "Have you never heard a woman come before, Two?"

"Not usually a priority of mine," Two confesses, no hint of a lie. "Not usually... fitting for the occasion."

"It's easy to make a woman cry," I interrupt because if he says another word, I'll smash his skull into the table. "If you're bigger, stronger, you can overpower them. Causing them pain, forcing them, that part's easy, and they console themselves afterwards that they had no choice. They can take comfort in their pain."

Three leans closer, listening to the words I'm spewing like I'm about to reveal some hidden secret when all I'm trying to do is stop myself from vomiting.

"But... If you can give them pleasure while taking yours, it's confusing. It makes them question everything. When Rachel sees me tomorrow, her mind will hate me, but her body... well, her body will remember every second of pleasure it felt. And that, lads, is a hundred times more torturous than any pain I could inflict on her."

They burst out laughing, and I smile along with them. Every word I said... fuck... true but not. That's likely how Rachel will feel in the morning, but it wasn't planned. All I wanted was to make her mine again. Still, my smile is genuine because these bastards sucked up every word, which keeps us all safe.

"You're a twisted fucker," Three says, pulling his phone from his pocket. "And you need to check your missed calls. The boss is after you."

Closing the kitchen door, I walk to the bottom of the garden. Two and Three are safe to leave alone because everyone else is locked in their rooms, and I hold the keys. Rachel has one for hers, and I have the spare, but Grace and Jeremy haven't been afforded the same *luxury. They're tied to the bedpost, and I have zero fucks to give about it. Miserable hypocrites.*

Pulling on the last of my cigarette, I crush it to the ground and light another. I'm gonna need it. My phone has three missed calls from Tony, all from when I was with his daughter. Taking a calming drag, I hit call before I bottle it.

"One," he says a second later. "You didn't answer."

"I was… busy."

"Right… and?"

And what? Does he want a play-by-play? Clearing the tar from my throat, I answer, "It's done."

The silence lasts a lifetime. "Is she—"

"She knows," I blurt out because this is officially the most awkward conversation I've ever had.

"Knows what?" Tony asks, though the threat in his voice suggests he understands.

"I thought it would be easier for her if she knew it was me… she figured the rest out."

"Nate…" Tony inhales a breath through his gritted teeth.

"Would you rather I hurt her? Traumatise her? That was my fucking alternative." I let that statement hang there, hoping he'll digest it and see I made the best choice. Standing up to Tony isn't something I do often. I love him, but there's also a healthy dose of respect and fear.

"Can you control her?" he finally asks.

"Yes." There's more confidence in my words than his. "She won't do anything to risk those girls getting hurt. But you—"

"Yeah," Tony chuckles. "I'm in for a severe kicking."

Exhaling a genuine laugh, memories of Rachel giving Tony an earbashing in the past still fresh in my mind—she and Trish were the only two who ever dared. "You and me both," I admit. Rachel may have been subdued when I left her, but I know her too well to expect that to last long.

"Nate?" Tony asks. The alarm in his voice sets bells ringing in me. "How do you think she'll react when you point a gun at her mum's head?"

Fuck.

"Do you think she'll keep calm then?"

Rachel wasn't supposed to be here. The plan was to have the girls hidden away, Two's and Three's guns on the grandparents, and mine on Trish. Tony wouldn't have it any other way, especially since my gun is the only one with real bullets. Two and Three are unaware they're carrying blanks. Tony's trust in them only stretches so far. Rachel can't know this because I need her to fear them. She needs to fall in line, which she will for the sake of her sisters, but when she sees us—me— aiming guns at the people she loves, I can't guarantee she won't let the cat out of the bag.

"I'll handle it. Don't worry."

"I trust you." Tony drops the call, unable or unwilling to hear more.

Turning, I face the house, looking up at the window of the room Rachel's sleeping in, an uncomfortable ache setting into my stomach. Rachel can't be in the room when shit goes down. It's too dangerous for everyone involved.

Sucking in more oxygen, I force the lingering doubts away. Tony trusts me for a reason, and I can control this. I have no choice.

Chapter Sixteen
Nate

Six Years Ago

"I want everyone at The Jockey at eight," Tony orders. "Give her the welcome home she deserves." He repositions a cushion on his sofa—a brand new cushion—for the tenth time, trying to make it look perfect.

Bobbie, his sister, took him shopping a few days ago to help him buy a ton of shit to make his house more feminine. This bruiser of a man didn't even know what a coaster was, but now he has two sets scattered around his living room.

"I'm all in a fucking tizz," he laughs, wiping his large hands, calloused from years spent running his

garage and beating the shit out of those who cross him, down his face. "I just want it to feel like it could be her home."

Never have I seen this man so on edge, so out of control, and all this because the 'her' in question is his daughter. Rachel's just turned eighteen, and she's finally returning to London—home. Tony's travelled up North to see her, but Trish has always refused to let Rachel come back here. Guess Rach wouldn't take no for an answer now that she's an adult.

It's been over two years since I last saw her, spoke to her... touched her, and I, like everyone else who works for Tony, am expected to celebrate at the pub later. It's just a visit, but Tony's hoping she may want to stay, especially as she's considering attending university here.

University. Fuck. She really did go on to live a different life.

"Alright, lad?" Tony nudges my arm, my focus moving from the cushion to him.

"Course," I lie. Truth is, I'm bricking it. Things with Rachel ended in the worst way possible. I finally had her—in every sense of the word—and then I allowed myself to be persuaded to let her go. For two years, I've subdued the 'what ifs' that plagued my thoughts, forced the guilt away. After she left, she called and texted all the time. First, she begged me to tell her dad to come and get her, insisting that her mum couldn't just take her away, but when I didn't reply, her messages changed. Pain and anger were etched into every word, her pleas for me to talk to her, to explain what she did wrong, why I didn't want her anymore.

Desperate to keep some connection, I read every message and listened to every voicemail on repeat until I couldn't take it anymore. I smashed my phone with a monkey wrench until there was nothing left but a shattered mess.

"Nate?" Tony brings me back to the present. "I don't know what the fuck I'm doing here. A bit of moral support wouldn't go amiss."

"Sorry..." Get it together. "The fuck do I know about interior decorating, but it looks OK to me."

Turning back to the sofa, Tony admires his work, a breathless nod confirming his agreement.

"Are you sure this is what she wants? The pub, I mean," I ask. "Does she want to see everyone?" Does she want to see me?

"Honestly, Nate. I don't know what the fuck she wants anymore." Grabbing my shoulder, Tony looks me in the eyes, a rare glimpse of vulnerability shining in his. "But whatever it is, I'll give it to her."

The pub is rammed with Tony's crew, and I make sure I interact with them all. I may have only just turned twenty, but I'm already Tony's 'go-to'—his second in command at the garage and on the streets. Everyone wants to greet me, a scrawny kid no more, and show their respect. I give them mine in return, but they're just a distraction; all I want to do is hide behind them.

Facing Rachel will either be like looking into a mirror, seeing the same turmoil in her heart that I've carried with me, or it will be like looking into a void—a black hole of emptiness and resentment.

"Oi, oi!" Tony calls as he walks through the door, and everyone cheers, pushes past me and blocks my view. Guess I got my wish. They all crowd around their princess, forcing me further back. They're so loud I can't hear her response, but I can imagine it. These are her dad's chosen men, and even though Tony kept her out of his business, he ensured she had the largest and most protective family around her as possible.

These guys have always doted on her. She'll be smiling, reciprocating their hugs, working her way through them all until Tony guides her to me.

It's only a matter of time before I come face to face with a personal reminder of how badly I fucked up. Every second, I feel her getting closer, my heart races, my palms sweat, and my guts are in knots. I need a distraction.

Spinning around, my eyes land on the pool table and the girl leaning against it, watching the scene unfold. Perfect. Lyssa's wary eyes are zoned in on Rachel, the tick in her jaw revealing her annoyance—or jealousy.

Without thinking it through, I stride over to her. "Lyssa..." Her head snaps to me, and her frown instantly disintegrates. "Looking gorgeous." It's not a lie. Just a slight exaggeration. With her blonde hair and bright blue eyes, she's nice to look at, and fuck—I've been here before—but when I look at her, it's like I can see it all. There's no mystery. Rachel wore her heart on her sleeve with me, but there always seemed to be so much hidden beneath, more truths to uncover.

Lyssa moves closer and reaches out, hooking her fingers around the hem of my shirt. "Nate... Been a while." Tilting her head towards the crowd, her eyes narrow. "Thought you'd be first in line."

"Nah." Grabbing her hand, I lead her to a table against the far wall, sink into the chair and scoop her onto my knee. "I'm good where I am, thanks."

Lyssa nuzzles into my neck, and her tongue darts out, leaving a hot trail of saliva across my throat. It makes me want to gag, so I close my eyes and breathe deeply, managing to make it seem like I'm enjoying it. There was a time when I did, but I stopped fooling around with Lyssa months ago when it was clear she wanted more than the occasional fuck. I've never committed to anyone, never fallen in love. Not since… Rachel.

The moment her name enters my head, the inevitable happens. Rachel reaches the last man, and they clear a path directly to me. In an instant, she goes from being filled with light to complete darkness. The smile she gave everyone else disappears. Hate-filled eyes stare me down, the fire in them so hot it burns a hole in my head. Falling further into the trap I've created for myself, I reach for Lyssa's hair and guide her face to mine. She moves in for a kiss, but I can't bring myself to do it. So, I use her as a shield from Rachel's judgment and contempt.

"What the fuck, Nate?" Tony barks, his tone laced with disappointment. "Couldn't—"

"Leave it, Dad." Rachel's voice cuts in. It's deeper and stronger than I remember, ringing out, full of confidence. The mere thought of my name rolling off her tongue has my dick twitching until she speaks again.

"He doesn't matter." Rachel's voice is so casual, you'd never know how sharp her words cut. "Alright, Lyssa?" she adds, and the burden on my lap spins around to face her, but remains seated. "Long time no see."

The fact that Rachel remembers Lyssa doesn't bother me. London is massive but tiny, depending on the circles you run in. It's Rachel's choice of words that hurt. She could've said, 'It doesn't matter,' but it's me. I don't matter to her.

"Well, you just up and left, didn't ya," Lyssa replies, still not standing to greet her properly, which is ballsy given Tony's present. "You look good," she adds begrudgingly, and I force my eyes to move from the back of Lyssa's head to Rachel's face.

My heart punches my chest, a warning to keep it safe. Rachel's completely and utterly gorgeous. The same but different. Older, wiser and wearing an oversized chip on her shoulder. Rachel doesn't look at me or thank Lyssa for her compliment; she just leans up onto her tiptoes to whisper into Tony's ear and then walks towards the toilet.

Tony glares at me, a silent warning of the earbashing I'll receive from him later before returning to the others. All I can do is stare at the door Rachel just walked through, wondering what the fuck to do next.

"Still a fucking bitch, then," Lyssa mutters under her breath.

Shoving her off my knee, not giving a single fuck if she loses her balance and falls flat on her face, I look her dead in the eye. "Yes. You are."

"Where the fuck is she?"

Tony looks panicked. It's been ten minutes since Rachel walked off, and he's freaking out.

"I'll go check." Placing my pint on the table, I head off before Tony can object. He decided not to wait too long to bollock me for repeating past mistakes and not giving Rachel the welcome I ought to —'Given how close we used to be.' If only he knew.

Pushing through the door Rachel walked through, I stop, realising I didn't think this through. I've got the gents' on my right, the ladies' further down on the left, and the door leading to the beer garden straight ahead. Slowly, like a man on death row, heading towards his fate, I walk down the corridor, prepared to barge straight into female territory, only to give myself whiplash when my head snaps towards the exit on hearing a familiar sound.

Rachel's laugh is imprinted on my soul. It was always a mission of mine to make her laugh at least once whenever I saw her, no matter how fleeting the *visit. It's not me she's laughing for now, though, and the jealousy has me barging into the beer garden, almost taking the door off its hinges.*

My entrance gets the attention of everyone, and when I finally locate her, she stops laughing. Rachel's cold stare stays locked on me as she takes a drag of the spliff between her fingers—I can smell it from here. Sparks of heat turn the cherry alight, and the fire in me turns demonic as I watch, frozen, as she sucks in the smoke and holds it.

"Steady on, gorgeous," a familiar voice laughs next to her.

Rachel turns to him, gives him a heart-shattering smile and exhales the drugs into the world before passing back the spliff.

"What. The fuck?" I grind out, storming over.

"Naaate," Leon smiles, too stoned to see the danger. "Rachel's come to visit."

"We're just catching up," Rachel adds, reaching for the spliff Leon is passing back to her, but I grab his wrist in a vice-like grip before she can take it.

"Do you think giving drugs to Tony Cannock's daughter is a good idea?"

"Relax, man. We—"

"Yeah, Nate." Rachel mocks, lifting the spliff from Leon's fingers. "Relax. They're my dad's drugs anyway... aren't they?" She winks at Leon, a flirtatious smile creeping past her lips—lips that once begged me to sink my teeth into them.

Knocking the spliff from her fingers, I grab Leon's jacket and yank him to his feet. The cunt finally has the sense to look afraid. "I'll deal with you later," I promise before dropping him back on his seat.

Gripping Rachel's arm, I pull her up a little less forcefully and drag her inside, ignoring her protests until we're alone in the corridor.

"What's your fucking problem?" she spits at me as I push her against the wall.

"You!" I bite back. "You are my problem, Rach. You waltz off and get high with the first dealer you meet."

"I know Leon from school, you twat!" Rachel shoves me away, but I bounce right back, keeping my body mere inches away from her—it doesn't faze her. "And I'm well aware that anyone dealing in this pub is doing so with my dad's approval."

"He wouldn't want you doing—"

"Oh, please. He has no idea what I have or haven't done over the past two years." Rachel pauses in her rant, then smiles, an idea forming in her mind. "Maybe I should start sharing with him more. What do you think, Nate?"

The threat lingers between us, but it's weaker than the undeniable tension. There may be hatred in her eyes, but there's want—need—there, too.

Leaning closer, my rage drawn to her fire. There's never been a push and pull with Rachel, only ever a pull. Magnets, always needing to be as close as possible. Seems two years of cold turkey haven't changed that. "Go for it. You stink of weed. He won't believe you."

"You saying he'll take your word over mine?" Pain shines in her eyes as the tears start to build up. "He cares more about you than me now. That's what you're saying?"

It wasn't, but it would be helpful if she thought that. I've never been able to see Rachel hurting— always felt her torment like it was my own. The protector in me wants to take it all away, but the survivor in me needs her to believe that what she's saying is true, so she doesn't go and run her mouth.

"Do you dare find out?" I challenge, holding her gaze, praying she'll blink first.

She does.

Forcing me away, Rachel shoves me into the wall. "I'm so done with this place." Going on the attack was always easier for her than letting the pain in. "Go back to whatever you were doing before I got here, and I'll go back to forgetting you exist."

Storming into the bar area, Rachel glides straight past Tony, causing him to race after her. The pub turns silent, everyone looking at me, wondering what the fuck has happened. Rachel's voice can be heard as she shouts in the streets, along with Tony's deeper tones, attempting to calm her. Torn between joining them and staying rooted to my spot, all eyes remain on me until the door opens. Tony goes to the group he was with and collects his coat. He doesn't even look my way as he says his goodbyes, but then he walks in my direction, stopping half a metre from me.

Slowly, his gaze meets mine, and I see the man I love more than I ever did my real dad, looking like he's torn in half. "She wants to go home."

Broken. That's the word that sums Tony up, and I know when Rachel said 'home', she meant Nottingham, not his place.

"I have a feeling there are some things we might need to talk about, Nate."

Taking a deep breath in, I force my eyes to remain on his; it's my best chance of figuring out how much shit I'm in.

"But for now," Tony continues. "I have just one thing to ask you."

Nodding, I prepare myself for what's to come.

"Did you break my little girl's heart?"

This time, I can't meet his eyes, and I stare at my feet, praying to whoever might listen to me that I won't lose him, too. Rising to meet his gaze, I tell the truth for the first time this evening. "Not intentionally."

Stepping closer, the whiskey coating his tongue fills the air, and I know I'm about two seconds away from getting what I'm owed. Tony's hand grips my shoulder, and it takes all my strength not to flinch. Tony's taught me much in life, including how to handle situations like this, so I do what's expected and keep my eyes on him. What I see isn't what I expected. A softness—understanding—like things suddenly make sense.

Inhaling what might be my final breath, my eyes turn to the door where Rachel now stands, watching the scene unfold before her. A flurry of emotions race across her face—none of them good.

"One more question…" Tony brings my attention back to him. "Did she break yours?"

Chapter Seventeen
Rachel

Present

The water scalds me as it blasts against my neck and chest. I should've showered last night before I got in bed with the girls, but I was physically, emotionally, and mentally done. If only exhaustion helped me sleep... it didn't. Nate's aroma—his and mine mixed together—invaded my senses all night. It was like consuming him again and again each time I inhaled.

Fear kept me awake, too. No matter how distant, every sound felt like a threat, and I swear I heard someone put pressure on the bedroom door. Nate promised we'd be safe and the other two would stay away, but how the hell can I trust him?

He let me down in the worst way possible, and then told me it was for my benefit. Just like fucking me senseless on repeat last night was for my sake, not his. This whole situation is such a head fuck. I'd struggle to believe it wasn't a dream, were it not for the ache all over my body. Oh, and the fact that I woke up squashed between the twins in their grandparents' house.

The icing on the cake? My dad is behind it all. The same dad who made me his princess and then sent me away. That's what he did. The weekend of my eighteenth birthday, he went from a doting dad to a distant memory. 'Maybe you shouldn't move back to London,' he'd said the morning after it all kicked off in the pub.

I know what I saw. He was comforting Nate when my heart was breaking. Even if the conversation Nate says he had with my mum is true, Dad knew nothing about it. He chose Nate over me, and now he's attacking Mum—what other explanation is there?

"Why is the bedroom door locked, Rachie?" Ivy asks, knocking on the shower door and making me jump out of my bright red skin. She's hidden by all the steam, and I'm Nate-free, so I step out of the shower and wrap a towel around myself.

Bella stands behind her sister, arms crossed over her chest, clearly disgruntled. Their spirit and tenacity are the kick up the arse I need to stop wallowing and see this shit through. Thoughts of shoving a kitchen knife into Nate's gut grace my mind, but the only truth I know is that doing as he says is our best chance of getting through this unscathed. If I have to fuck him again, I will—for their sake. Definitely not because he gave me the four best orgasms I've ever had in my life.

Pushing images of his ridiculously delicious cock pumping into me far out of my mind, I focus on the girls, who are getting more impatient by the second. "One only wants us to come downstairs when everything's ready." Turning away, I hide the lie by opening the cupboard above the sink, thankful that Grace always keeps the en-suite well-stocked, ready for when they entertain.

Bella tugs at the towel as I spray a decent amount of deodorant under each pit. "We don't want to play anymore!"

"Can we go to yours?" Ivy chimes in.

"I told you. Mummy and Daddy have paid for them to help."

Rubbing moisturiser into my face, I chance a look at their reflections, finding that they're doing their twin thing—silently communicating or hatching a plan. Neither is good because when these two decide on something, they'll do whatever it takes to get it. If that means kicking up a massive fuss to the point where Grace and Jeremy insist we leave, which has worked in the past, they'll try it. Only this time, they won't succeed. Grace and Jeremy aren't in charge.

Facing them both, I kneel on the floor to get level with them. "Listen…" Wiggling my finger, I beckon them closer. "Who do you think hates being stuck in this house more than you?"

Devious grins spread across their faces, and they both point at me. They may have overheard me bitching about their grandparents once or twice.

"Exactly. Sooo… if I can manage to do it for one more day and night, can't you?" Their silence doesn't inspire confidence. "I promise to make it fun, and One will as well. We can bake, paint, build dens, play hide and seek, and there's waaay more space here than in my flat."

"Knock, knock."

We all jump when we see Nate… no One, standing in the doorway to the ensuite, mask in place. The girls frown, and I stand tall, pulling my towel even tighter.

"Didn't mean to scare you." One's boyish grin sets them at ease, but my desire to punch him grows stronger each second. "Your grandparents are downstairs. Why don't you go and join them?"

"Can we wait for Rachel?" Bella asks.

One's eyes glide over my body at an agonisingly slow pace, his tongue flicking across his lower lip, reminding me how it felt when he was devouring my clit. "Rachel's not ready yet, and I have some secrets to share with her about today."

"Secrets?" They giggle with glee.

"Told you we'll make it fun." Playing along, I raise a foot and give them both a gentle nudge forward, One following them out of the room.

Already knowing he's not going to let me off that easily, I reach for my dress from yesterday and yank it over my head, holding the towel at my chest until I can get my bra. Seconds later, he walks back into the ensuite and places the key to the bedroom in his pocket. When his hand resurfaces, it's holding a pair of black cotton knickers.

Dangling them in the air, the smug and satisfied slant of his jaw has my blood pressure rising to murderous levels again. "Thought you might appreciate a fresh pair."

One makes no attempt to move, so I reluctantly reach for them. "You are quite literally wearing granny pants," he snorts a laugh, and I snatch them off him, ditch my towel and pull them on, doing my best not to let him see more of me than he deserves.

"Had a wank over Grace's underwear drawer, did you?" I refuse to let him make me laugh, even though his happiness was always infectious. My loner next door—the poor lad being beaten by his dad. My crush, my heart, my everything... I still remember the first time he properly smiled for me. It hadn't taken much. All I'd done was ask him to.

No Rachel. Fuck that shit, and fuck him.

Smile still fixed in place, One steps towards me. "Jealous?"

"I'm not in the mood for games." Glaring at him seems to stop him from coming any closer, so I keep my anger in place like his mask is. "You do realise how hard today will be, right? The girls don't want you here, and they don't want to be here. I can keep them busy, but they're gonna hit a wall at some point."

"None of us got much sleep last night. Two are Three are wound tight." Moving closer, One grips both my arms, holding me in place. "Grace and Jeremy

will behave, the girls are just kids, but you, Rach."
Leaning closer, he nudges his nose against mine,
jolting the darkest parts of me awake. "Can I trust you
to keep your head?"

"I know what's at stake," I snap, but I don't move
away.

"Good." Warm fingers grip my jaw. "In the eyes
of my partners, I claimed you last night. I forced
something on you that you didn't want—"

"I didn't want it," I fume. Whatever I felt, I
wouldn't have chosen to fuck him last night, given a
better option.

Ignoring me, he tightens his hold. "They will
expect you to submit to me, and if you don't, they will
question why."

Forcing a swallow, I free myself from his grip, but
he continues. "I have my role, and you have yours.
You're not Princess Rach—"

"Fuck off!"

"You're my toy." One backs me into the wall,
watching me as his words sink in. "Keep hold of that
hate… you'll need it."

Chapter Eighteen
Rachel

"What are you staring at?"

Grace flinches at my words, but it's been two hours, and I can't take her silent judgment any longer. Walking into the kitchen was the hardest thing I've ever done. Two and Three raked their eyes over my body, and I instantly felt ashamed, knowing everyone in the room would've heard me come last night. For the first time since I can remember, I felt dirty. If Two and Three were so pleased with the situation, surely it was wrong? They're sick in the head.

All I did was involuntarily orgasm. Still, with all eyes on me, One felt like my only ally, so when he pulled out a chair and gestured for me to sit, I complied. Since then, I've done everything he's asked, like the good submissive he told me to be, but I can't take Grace's eyes on me any longer.

"You know we're only in this mess because of your lies and greed, don't you?" I snap, keeping my voice low. The girls are on good form at the moment, and I don't want to change that. Nor do I want Two or Three to get involved.

"Ladies," One warns from beside me at the table. It's just the three of us here since Jeremy's using his allocated toilet break, with a masked man in tow.

Grace stutters, her eyes unable to meet mine. "I know... I. I... I'm sorry."

"What? You're apologising. To me?" This has never happened the entire time she's been in my life. If ever she's done something to offend in the past, she's found a way to make it my fault.

Lifting her chin, she finally meets my gaze, her eyes reflecting not judgment but guilt. "Yes." For the briefest moment, Grace looks over to One, and I know what she's apologising for.

One leans forward, his elbows resting on the table. "Something you'd like to say to me, Grace?" His tone is light, but the threat lingers beneath.

Grace hears it and shakes her head; her hair, slightly greasy, covers her face, and I can't decide if I feel sorry for her fear or that she's never looked so unkempt.

"Don't be shy, Grace," One pushes. "This is your home. By all means, say how you feel."

"Leave!" Grace shouts, startling me.

"All in good time," One stares her down, remaining calm. His soft tone, a stark contrast to his stance.

"Then leave Rachel alone," she demands, finding her strength from somewhere. "Don't... don't do that to her again."

"Oh..." One leans back against his chair and reaches over to me. His hand rests on my shoulder, his fingers lazily twirling my hair. "That." One pauses, and Jeremy and Two return to the room.

"Bit frosty in here, One," Two quips. "Are you losing your touch?"

"Never." It takes half a second for One to scoop me up and pull me onto his lap, causing me to yelp in shock.

My back's pressed against his chest, and I have a front-row seat to Grace and Jeremy's reactions. Jeremy looks anywhere but at me, but for half a second, it seems like Grace might fight for me.

"You know what, Grace?" One states. "There's not a single photograph of Rachel in this house."

"Bollocks," Two scoffs.

"Oh... I've checked," One replies. "Lots of the twins, your son and his doting wife. But Rachel... nada." His hand wraps around my throat, lightly gripping so he can tilt my head to the side, exposing my neck to him. Heated breath caresses my skin, sending jolts of pleasure down my spine. The pulse in his wrist presses against my neck, raging, reminding me of the boy who once stood up to a group of five lads on the estate when they tried to lift my school skirt and peek underneath. It had taken him hours to calm down that night, and every time I touched him, I thought his heart was going to explode.

Stop going there. He's not that boy anymore.

"I'm not their granddaughter," I offer with no idea why I'm defending them.

"Not by blood, no. But how long have you been in their lives now?" One's grip tightens the angrier he gets. I should hate it, hate him, but I don't. His touch should repulse me, manhandling me in front of these people. It doesn't. Just like when he pressed me against the wall last night when I had no clue who he was, my body acts on its own accord, begging for more—what, I'm not sure. Danger, love, pleasure, pain... life.

You're dead on the inside.

"We... just—" Grace splutters, a welcome distraction to my spiralling thoughts.

"Who is your dad, Rachel?" Two asks, preventing Grace from defending herself.

One's once raging pulse momentarily stops before beating again, stronger but slower, a warning I hear ringing in my ears.

"He's a nobody," I lie, grabbing One's wrist and freeing my neck. "Barely even remember what he looks like."

"That so?" Two asks, his bored tone failing to hide the intrigue in his eyes.

"Yes," I grit out, staring him down. "Turns out he had another family... preferred having a son to a daughter."

Pushing myself off One's knee, I spin and face him, his mask doing nothing to hide his rage and contempt. He can't stand it when I say shit about my dad, never could, and it must be killing him that he can't argue back.

It's tempting to push him again, but all mention of my dad clears the One... the Nate-scented fog from my brain, and I remember to play my part. I'm supposed to be afraid. So, instead of making my demands, I make a simple request, the thing I need more than anything right now.

"One... Can I go and check on my sisters, please?"

Chapter Nineteen
Nate

It's been two hours since Rachel left the kitchen. Having followed her to the living room where Three was watching the girls, I ensured he understood the boundaries and left her to it. It's been hell, and I've kept silent, listening to every sound made. Still, Rachel knows her sisters better than I do, and if they don't want us around, I'll give them all some space. Best not to crowd them with masked men and risk a meltdown.

Three. Fucking. Hours. That's all this job was meant to be. Everything would've been golden, no hassle. The kids would've been appropriately entertained and kept out of the way for the grand finale. The only plus to the extended stay is that I have Rachel with me, but that's both a silver lining and a complete nightmare.

Truth is, this is boring as fuck. We're just killing time, keeping things quiet. It's not like we brought entertainment with us, and this hideous kitchen chair is making my arse numb. Rising, I stretch my arms. "It's nearly lunchtime. I'll go and get Rachel."

The second I turn away from the table, I hear two high-pitched squeals coming from the living room.

"What the—"

"Stay," *I order Two. Picking up my pace, I'm seconds from the door when I hear another scream.*

"Don't you fucking dare!"

Rachel... Shit!

Barging through the door, I see Three raising his fist; his other hand is snaked through Rachel's hair, keeping her in place. The slam of the door against the wall gets Three's attention, and his head turns to me. Rachel uses the distraction to smash her right fist into Three's wrist, causing him to yell in pain and release her hair.

That's my girl.

Three rights himself and prepares to close the space between them, but I get there first, and his fist stops an inch from my face, stuck in my bone-crushing hold. The twins are crying, but I don't turn to look. If they saw my eyes right now, it'd make things even worse. Everything in me is screaming murder. I told Rachel to keep it together, but I'm the one who might ruin it all. There's always been an unwritten rule in Tony's crew: Hurting Rachel comes with an immediate death sentence. Not because he told us, but because we all just fucking loved her so much—me more than anyone.

Keep control.

"Explain." That's all I manage through my gritted teeth.

"She fucking had it coming," Three argues.

Slowly, I release his wrist—I'm supposed to be on his side, after all. "Not yours to touch."

"She came at me," he spits; the visible parts of his face are bright red.

"Not yours to punish," I add, my tone deadly. "Step back." He doesn't move. "Step. Back." Pointing to the number on my chest as I speak, I remind him of the pecking order, and he finally relents.

Satisfied with the distance, I turn to face Rachel. She's shaking, and tears are ready to spill over—it's her fury seeping out, not her fear. Gripping her arms, I demand the same thing of her. "Explain."

Jaw clenched, she tries to turn to her sisters, but I jerk her, forcing her to keep her eyes on me. "They just wanted to go outside," she forces out.

"And I said no," Three fumes from behind me.

"I was trying to explain that to them when that prick—"

"Try again," I interrupt. "Using your nice words."

Rachel's eyes widen, her venom now focused on me, and I do my best to remind her with my pleading stare of the roles we must play.

"I was trying to help," she continues more softly, causing my heartbeat to relax. "But then he yelled, they got upset, and he threatened them."

"Bollocks," Three protests.

136

"He said he'd give them something to cry about!"

"And you protected them," I conclude on Rachel's behalf, and she nods. Releasing her arms, I pull her against my chest and turn her so that she now has her back to Three. Keeping my voice low, I tell her, "Put a smile on your face, and tell those girls to hide upstairs."

"What?" Her voice is muffled against my hoodie, but I hear the uncertainty.

"It's game time," I announce to the room.

Pulling away, she stares at me, trying to work out what's happening. Using my mask to my advantage, I keep my mind blank and my face neutral because if she could tell what I was thinking—even get a slight inkling—she'd lose her shit.

"Bella, Ivy," Rachel says, smiling brightly at the girls. She sure does know how to act when it comes to them. "Time for hide and seek."

"Come with us," Ivy requests, all sadness gone from her voice.

Facing them, I notice that both have stopped crying. Did they play us? It's clear they're determined little things, just like their big sister, but this isn't an argument they can win. "Rachel and I are going to have some quiet time, and after you've hidden, Two is going to come and find you." They still look unconvinced.

"If it takes him longer than five minutes to find you, he'll give you some of those posh biscuits Grandma hides," Rachel smiles, knowing exactly how these girls work.

137

It does the trick, and they sprint out of the room within seconds.

"Go stand by the door," I order Three, and with a huff, he does as he's told. "We don't want to be disturbed," I add with a devilish grin, instantly appeasing him.

Focusing on Rachel, I step back and stare her down. She was relieved when the girls left, but now there's a hint of confusion dancing in those hypnotic doe eyes. "After last night, I thought you understood the importance of being my good girl."

Rachel shifts on her feet, no clue how to respond.

"A good girl wouldn't attack my friend."

"And a real man doesn't threaten children!" she snaps, pointing towards Three.

"That's true..." Raising my finger, I stop Three's comeback before it has a chance to leave his mouth. "But you still broke the rules, and when rules are broken, bad girls get to beg for forgiveness."

"I won't apologise," she grits out, foolishly playing right into my hands.

Having her here at my mercy again is doing things to me that it shouldn't because I do want to fucking punish her. I don't give a fuck about Three, but the shit she spewed in the kitchen needs answering for. Calling Tony a nobody after everything he gave up for her, still failing to understand the depths of his love. Yes. I'm going to shut her up once and for all.

"I don't need you to say a word, sweet Rachel. I need you on your fucking knees."

"Wha-what?"

Taking out my gun, I ensure the safety is on before using it to gesture that she should lower to the ground. "You're not sorry, so your words mean nothing. What I need is for you to prove your obedience to me."

"One—"

"Knees," I bark, and finally, I break through to her.

Slowly, eyes on me the whole time, communicating the only way she can just how badly I'll pay for this, both knees meet the floor.

"That's more like it," Three croons.

"I don't want to hear a single sound from you," I throw at Three before turning back to face the devil in a submissive's robe, waiting for my next instruction. Placing the gun in the pocket of my hoodie, I step in front of Rachel and release my already hard cock from its restraints.

Rachel's mouth parts on a gasp, her eyes darting from my dick to my face. She pales, realising this is going to happen, but there's no hint of an objection. Mere minutes ago, she got a taste of what Three was prepared to do to her. Had I not stepped in, he'd have knocked her down and dragged her out of that room to finish her off. My prior claim void because she lashed out first.

"Does he need to be here?" she croaks out.

The fact that it's the audience she's objecting to and not sucking my dick makes it even harder. I never got to fuck her mouth—time to right that wrong. "Three needs to see that you can be good, Rachel." Bending over, I hover by her ear and whisper, "It's only you and me… You and me."

Her hot breath burns my skin as she exhales deeply, but she consents with a slight nod.

"Don't worry. I've washed it since I took you last night," I tell her with a smile, and it's true. "And if you get tempted to sink your teeth in… to be a bad girl…" She sucks in a breath. "You'll die choking on my blood." Not true, but the approving chuckle from Three shows that it had the desired effect.

Gripping my cock, I raise my chin at her. "What's it going to be, Rachel?"

Rising, Rachel's mouth is mere centimetres from my cock, her tongue creeps out, and she wets her lips, eyes focused on my dick like she can't wait to devour it—or bite it off—that's still a possibility—she slowly lifts her eyes to mine. "I'll be good."

No further coaxing needed. Rachel opens wide and takes me deep. No, messing around, no teasing my tip; she takes my entire cock to the back of her throat until her nose presses against my pelvis.

"Jesus. Fucking. Christ," I gasp, gripping her hair and holding her there for a moment longer. Eyes closed, I need another second to ground me, to clench my muscles and control the pleasure. Guiding her head back, I feel her inhale through her nose, and it both amazes and kills me that she's so fucking good at this.

A slight grunt from Three pulls me out of the black hole that imagining who Rachel's been with sends me down, and I hear the sound of him tugging at his dick before I tune him out. Eyes open, I look down at Rachel and see the satisfaction in her eyes, and I remember that I planned to punish her, not succumb to her.

Rachel's mouth slides up, but the moment she tries to release my cock, I force her head back down, appeased when she releases an involuntary gag. It takes only a second for her to interpret the look in my eyes, the flexing in my jaw, to realise that she has indeed been bad, and I'm absolutely going to punish her.

Hands either side of her head, I cover her ears. The only thing I'll spare her from is having to listen to Three wanking himself off. Besides that, she deserves what's coming, and she knows it. She can't move, can't control the pace. She's not going to be sucking my dick, I'm going to be fucking her face.

Slowly, I pull back, then slam forward, hitting her throat. A hiss escapes my lips. One consolation for Rachel is that this isn't going to last long. Again, I pull back and slam forward; Rachel's teeth grazing my cock whenever she gags on it, adding to the pleasure.

Tears stream down her cheeks. "You really are a good girl," I praise. Pulling out, I'm teetering at the edge of explosion. "And I'm going to reward you by letting you swallow my cum."

"Fuck-ah!" Three murmurs, and I know he's just spunked all over himself, a sickening vision that does little to deter me at this point. Rachel's all I see, and her greedy eyes tell me she wants all of me.

Pushing further in, I increase my grip on her hair. "Ready?"

Rachel gives a slight nod in response. Pulling back, I smash into her two more times before my cum is flowing down her throat.

"Fuck yes," I groan, my balls spasming, lightning striking down my spine. My heavy, hooded eyes open to see Rachel looking up at me, an emotion in her eyes I can't place. Am I delusional to think it's lust? That this scenario gave her pleasure? Wishful thinking, no doubt. She's more likely to be plotting my death.

"I'm going to pull out now. No spills," I warn her. Sliding out, I smear the cum from the tip of my cock around her lips, and her tongue immediately follows the trail, licking it all up.

So. Fucking. Hot.

Gently dragging the tip of my finger along her jawline, I keep my eyes on hers. "I knew you could be good, Rachel." Silent and stunned, Rachel leans back, resting against her heels, and I tuck my still-hard cock back into my trousers.

Striding over to Three, he, thankfully, has tucked his away, too, the look on my face, killing the smile creeping past his crooked teeth. "Go and get cleaned up. Take over from Two in the kitchen and have him go and find the twins."

"One," he nods—apparently, I've stunned him into obedience too—and turns to open the door.

"One more thing…" I add, and he freezes. "Touch Rachel or threaten the girls again, and you'll be sucking Two's cock. Got it?"

As soon as he's gone, I inhale a few times, filling my lungs with more air than necessary before turning to face Rachel. She's in the same position as before, staring at the wall, breathing hard.

Kneeling low, I cup her chin and lean in. She still doesn't move, so I use the moment to brush kisses along her jawline, leaving goosebumps in my wake. "Keep your shit together, Rach," *I gently warn.* "Because if you put me in that position again, I will bend you over and take you up the arse in front of both of them. Got it?"

Chapter Twenty
Rachel

"What the fuck is wrong with you?" I whisper-shout at my reflection. It's been hours since I got off the floor, dragged myself to the downstairs toilet and washed my face.

If only that were all.

My jaw ached, my throat was sore, and my throbbing core was soaked. Staring at the swollen lips of the stranger gawking back at me, wondering what the fuck happened—like I still am—my hand moved on its own accord, snaked under my dress, into Grace's underwear, and grazed my swollen clit.

Rubbing hard, showing myself the same level of mercy that Nate showed my mouth—absolutely none—I ripped a silent orgasm from my body and then joined everyone in the kitchen as if nothing happened.

Was it being watched? I don't think so. Nate's hands blocked out any other sound, making us the only people in the room. I forgot Three was even there. As much as I hate to admit it, the truth is, it was Nate. The way he pushed my limits, took away the control I always fought to keep—the control I thought I had.

Is that it? I let him have all the power—put myself at his mercy. For all my big words, it seems that nature won over nurture, and the type of man I've steered clear of since leaving London is the type of man I want—need. A man unafraid to anger me, to say no to me... to not allow me to say no. Did I even want to?

For the rest of the afternoon and evening, I spoke only when spoken to unless the girls needed more from me. Like the night before, Nate guided me around the kitchen, preparing dinner, my sick self, craving every moment of his touch. Now, the girls are asleep, and my knees are shaking in anticipation of what happens next. It's nerves... it must be. I can't possibly want Nate to fuck me again. Scrap that. It's rage. I'm furious that he forced a blowjob out of me, and I'm desperate to see him alone so I can beat the shit out of him.

"Right," I scoff at myself and look at my flushed face. Even my reflection is mocking me.

"Knock, knock," a voice whispers, accompanied by a gentle tap on the bathroom door.

Yanking it open, I glare at Nate. No. He doesn't deserve that title—he's just One—and then shove him aside so I can see the girls. They're sound asleep, thankfully. They're bored and scared, and it took hours for them to nod off.

"You're needed," One exhales the words against my ear, then guides me by my elbow out of the room.

Once locked, we walk down the stairs in silence. My eyes find the door to the spare room, and my body aches again. Trust him, I remind myself, but when I hear two more male voices in the kitchen, my legs turn to lead. He wouldn't… I was good.

"Relax," One says, sensing my unease. "You're not in trouble."

Spell broken, I yank my elbow from his grip, and my nails dig into my palms as I fight the urge to punch him. All he does is laugh, and I can do nothing in return because, in just one more step, we'll be in the kitchen with the others.

One pushes the door open, revealing a pale, terrified Grace with Two and Three on either side of her, guns on the table, in easy reach. "Sit," One orders, pulling out my chair before placing my phone in front of me. The notification that I've had three missed calls lights up the screen… all from Mum. Shit.

"Now…" One pulls my attention to him. "You've proven you can be a good girl today, but this is a biggie, so we're keeping Grace close to ensure you stay focused."

"What do you need?" I ask, my voice vacant because I already know the answer. Putting on an act in front of the girls is one thing, but Mum can smell my bullshit a mile away. One wrong word, or the right word in the wrong tone, will get her suspicious. That's not the worst of it. Every part of me wants to scream at her not to come here. To stay where she is, far away *and safe. I can't, though, because that move would kill us all.*

"We need you not to do anything fuckin' stupid," Three replies.

"Call her," One steps in, ignoring him. *"Look at me."* I do. *"The call will be on speaker phone; I will hear everything. If your mum gets suspicious, people die. If Grace opens her mouth, Grace dies... after watching her husband die."*

My eyes dart to Grace, and even though every inch of her is shaking, she doesn't even squeak. "I get it." I exhale deeply, forcing the nerves from my body. "I can play my part."

"Tell me what's been happening this weekend," One orders.

"I've been looking after the twins because Grace and Jeremy are ill," I reply on cue.

"That's right. Now, before you call her back, I'll fill you in on a few things," One states, so matter of fact. *"Your mum knows you're here because you told her in a text message yesterday."*

"Why did I do that?" My cheeks flush, fury building at the realisation that he's been through my phone.

"Because last time Grace spoke to her son, she told him she had plans this weekend, and the girls will be with you."

"Can't have the stars of the show going to the wrong venue, can we?" Two adds, his sickening smile spreading across his face.

"Indeed." One taps my phone, my cue to act.

Fingers shaking, I unlock the screen, pull in more oxygen than needed, give Grace a reassuring nod, and then make the call. The foreign ringtone sounds out across the kitchen for just one beat before I hear her voice.

"Finally! I was getting worried."

Nothing... my mouth opens, but nothing comes out.

"Rachel?" Mum's panicked voice echoes in my ears, close but distant, but the sight of Three's hand moving closer to his gun reconnects my brain.

"Here... yes, sorry, Mum. I was putting the girls to bed when you called." Keeping my eyes on the phone, I block everyone else out, although One's grip on my leg silently reminds me to keep it together.

"Bit late," Mum comments, but I can't handle the small talk.

"When are you back?"

"Rach..." Mum exhales. "I'm so sorry you got dragged into this. You weren't supposed to be there."

What? One's words slam into me. He spoke those exact words to me, and the deja vu knocks me off kilter.

"Johnson didn't tell me about staying longer until he'd called his parents," she continues, and my pulse slows down again. "I'm so sorry your weekend's been ruined. It's one thing to have the girls last minute, but Grace and Jer—"

A manic, uncontrolled giggle escapes my mouth involuntarily, but I quickly stifle it. If only this were just a ruined weekend. "It's fine, honestly," I force out, sounding more normal than ought to be possible.

"How is everyone?" She sounds hesitant but knows how I feel about her in-laws, so it's understandable.

Playing along is my only option. "Grace and Jeremy are terrible patients; nothing I do is good enough, and the girls are desperate to see you. But... but other than that, it's fine."

Mum laughs, and the distortion on the line makes it sound inhuman, and her next words are too garbled to understand.

Stay away. Don't come back. "When will you get here?" I ask, desperate to end this nightmare. Every word spoken feels like I'm betraying her.

"We should be there by 10:30," she sighs. "Just one more night to get through, sweetheart."

"Yeah... one more night."

"I am sorry, Rachel," she adds more firmly. "And I bloody love you."

My chest tightens, my throat constricts, and tears fill my eyes. I just need to tell one truth amongst the sea of lies spoken, and then she'll be gone. "I bloody love you too."

One hangs up the call for me, and I gasp for air. Tears burn my eyes, my blood pulsing as fear and rage take hold. This is all his fault. Glaring at One, my teeth grinding, using all my strength not to blow our cover, I unleash the only way I can. "Any other snooping you'd like to confess?"

One rises from his seat, staring me down. "Two. Three. Take Grace to her room, lock her up and find somewhere to sleep. I need clear heads tomorrow."

"Come now, Gracey," Two laughs. "The lovebirds are about to quarrel."

"Rachel," Grace whispers, a plea for me to back down that is disregarded.

"Nothing to worry about here, Grace," One cooes, his tone calmer than the look in his eyes. "Rachel is aware of the consequences if she misbehaves again."

"Fuck. You." The words leave me without thought. It's all too much. The reality is sinking in that tomorrow morning, Mum will arrive, and this already fucked-up situation could get ten times worse. She's coming here. Stepping into the lion's den because I sat there and let it happen.

One steps closer, nostrils flared. "Oh, baby girl…" Grabbing my jaw, he jerks my head forward. "You read my mind."

Chapter Twenty-One
Rachel

Flying face-first onto the mattress, getting a nose full of the musky fluids One and I released over the sheets last night, I bounce a few times before rolling over onto my back. I thought I'd have the advantage and get into a fighting position while One locked the door, but I was wrong.

Launching himself onto the bed, he whips out some cable ties from his pocket, secures them around my wrist, yanks me up the bed and attaches them to the headboard. He's so fast, there's no time to speak, and seconds later, it's not possible to, as he shoves fabric into my mouth.

"I don't even know where to fucking start with you," One rages, his mouth an inch from my face. Legs

on either side of my body, he pins me in place with his weight.

Chest heaving, I wait for whatever he plans for me next since I'm helpless to stop it, but all he does is stare, his chest rising in pace with my own.

At last, he releases a long breath, and his shoulders relax. "I know what you just had to do was hard, but you have got to rein in your temper, Rach." The sincerity in his voice makes my chest ache, but not enough to quell the annoyance.

Caressing my cheek with his fingertips, a smile graces his lips. "Not gonna lie. It's nice to see that you're still you. Still a force to be reckoned with. Still fucking clueless."

Fighting against my gag, I try my best to respond but fail to force myself free of whatever he shoved into my mouth. Pulling against the restraints is just as hopeless, only causing the plastic to dig further into my skin.

"I'll remove them… eventually," he smirks. "I'm just trying to work out what to do with you." One rests an elbow beside my head and leans on his hand, studying me. "The stuff you believe about your dad is shit, but it's not my place to tell you his truths. As for your phone…" he pauses, relishing in the fact that he's about to piss me off. "Under the circumstances, it would be lax of me not to review the messages coming through, and I'm nothing if not thorough."

Winking, he shuffles to the side, and his body rests against mine. His free hand slides along my leg, teasing its way up to my underwear, and my core tingles in response. There's no way I'm letting him see what he does to me, so I remain like a stone, barely even blinking when deft fingers lift the fabric to one side and start gently rubbing my clit.

"You are so fucking beautiful when you're promising me death with your gaze," he chuckles. "Helpless. Bound. Completely at my mercy." Pressing his hard cock against my thigh, his mask scratches my neck as his teeth graze the sensitive skin by my ear. "Can you feel what you do to me, Rachel? You drive me crazy. You always did."

Two fingers push inside me, and I groan against the gag.

"Can you feel what I do to you, or are you too stubborn to admit you love it?"

Squeezing my eyes closed, I try to force him out of my head as my hips move in rhythm with his thrusting fingers.

"Were you this wet when you had my cock in your mouth?" he asks, and I groan at the memory. "Shall I free your mouth so I can fill it up?" More moans… I just can't help giving him what he wants.

"As much as I want to fuck your face again, I owe you one." One glides along my body, yanks my knickers down my legs and flings them across the room. Spreading my knees wide, he pulls off his mask and stares at my exposed cunt in awe. Leaning lower at an agonisingly slow pace, his nose nuzzles between my butt cheeks, and he licks his way from my puckered hole to my aching clit.

Arching my back, I follow his movements as he repeats the process. "Yummy..." He leans back to study me again, his thumb sending shivers up my spine as it rests against my rear.

I'm an open-minded girl, but I've only ever tried anal once, and my overenthusiastic partner ruined it for anyone who ever tried to breach that entrance again. Something tells me this will be different, and though I'd never say this out loud, I want One... Nate... to have every part of me.

"I did warn you that if you didn't behave, I'd take this hole, too." Jumping from the bed, he goes into the ensuite. The opening and closing of cupboard doors has me clenching my thighs together in anticipation, searching for more friction.

One returns with a tub of Vaseline and a devilish smile—trust Grace to keep her bathrooms stocked with everything. Right now, it makes me like her a little more.

One strips naked, his delicious cock dripping with pre-cum, then resumes his previous position on the bed and pulls my legs apart so he can dive face-first back into my core. His moans are as muffled as mine as he feasts on my pussy, fingers stretching me as he drives me closer to release.

"Have you ever?" he asks, a knuckle pressing against my rear. When I don't respond, he climbs up my body and pulls the rough fabric from my mouth. "Has anyone taken you up the arse before?"

Swallowing, I try to moisten my throat, deciding how to answer. "Loads of times," I croak out, and he sees the lie.

"Best make this one to remember, then."

Shit.

"Think you can keep your mouth shut?" he asks, dangling the fabric—a pair of pink cotton knickers—not mine—in front of my face, almost bringing my dinner back up. He tosses them to the floor. "You get one chance," he warns me. "One."

Pausing to ensure I understand the dual meaning of the word, he slides back down. He goes straight back to my clit, and I grip him with my thighs, keeping him in place as small gasps escape. My moans deepen when he pushes two fingers inside me, his thumb rubbing against my rear.

One. One. One. One. He mustn't be Nate.

"I need to be in here first," he groans. Lifting himself above me, One presses his cock against my wet pussy.

"Stop!" I scream, panic lacing my voice, and he freezes in place. "Condom," I add more calmly, finding my cool.

"You're on the pill."

"And when did I last take one?" I challenge. "When will I get a chance to take another?" That shiny purple pack is waiting for me at home, untouched since Friday morning.

One pauses momentarily, then pushes straight in, his mouth crashing into mine.

"Did you hear me?" I pant against his lips.

"I'm not going to come in this hole, Rachel. I need to feel you come on my dick again." Sliding one hand around my throat, he cuts off my next argument. Thrusting into me, hitting my g-spot whilst building up delicious friction when his pelvis grinds against my clit, he dips a finger into the Vaseline and presses it against my rear.

"Best get it ready for me." With no further warning, he pushes inside, and the burn has me gasping. Fingers still wrapped around my neck, he tilts my head, locking my eyes on his, our lips meeting with desperate kisses.

Another finger enters, stretching me further, sending my senses into overdrive as the pleasure, fire, and pressure build, creating a crescendo of chaos throughout my body. "Gah," I gasp, clenching around him.

"You like that, don't you? Daddy's little princess likes getting her arse fuck—"

My teeth sink into his bottom lip, cutting off his words. I may love what he's doing to me, but I've never been Daddy's princess.

Ignoring the pain, he starts scissoring the fingers in my butt. His eyes hold a challenge, lust, and the need to punish me all at once, and I watch him for as long as I can before the pleasure shooting through my body has me squeezing my eyes shut, my body shaking uncontrollably.

One kisses my forehead. "Good girl. You soaked me beautifully and managed to keep your mouth shut."

My eyes fly open as he slides out, fear now gripping me. He's big, and I shouted my mouth off before because I can't back down from a challenge, and although having him finger fuck my arse felt amazing, his dick will be another matter.

We stare at each other as he spreads Vaseline along his bare, engorged cock. Gently, his finger pushes back in, encouraging me to relax. "Last chance to tell me the truth."

The truth. Great. The truth may save my skin or give him more power, not that I have any right now, bound to this bed.

"Rachel..." His husky voice coaxes me back from my muddled thoughts. "Have I ever let you fall?"

Yes. He let me fall in love with him, leaving an unfillable void in my life. Yet, no. Not when it mattered most.

Swallowing hard, I take a deep breath in. "Once..." I exhale. "And it was horrible."

Nodding, he pushes another finger inside as his free hand rubs against my clit. "Is this horrible?"

Tilting my hips to get more friction, I shake my head.

"Relax," he encourages, then he leans lower and removes his thumb from my clit. Holding his dick in the palm of his hand, his fingers slide out, he pushes the tip inside, and my legs fly up in response to the burn that's ten times worse than before.

"Breathe," he orders, his face straining.

Closing my eyes, I focus on the friction building against my clit whilst relaxing my muscles, allowing him in deeper. Fuck, it hurts, but not in an unwelcome way. The pain dulls as every second passes, and the promise of pleasure rises.

"There you go." His strained tone attempts to soothe me. "Look how good you're taking me." Slowly, his hips move back and forth, savouring every second and easing me in. "Of course, you hated it last time. This body was made only for me."

"It… it feels… g-good," I gasp each syllable. "But I still fucking hate you."

Laughing, he moves faster. "You should really stick to using your nice words when you have my dick in your arse."

Sucking in more air, I adjust to the pace, the fullness, losing myself in the moans of pleasure one buries in the crook of my neck. I refuse to believe what he says—I'm not his. He's just exceptionally good at fucking, that's all.

Proving my point, an orgasm starts to build deep inside my core, heat spreading. As I begin to tremble, One's movements become more erratic, and as the first hint of a moan passes my lips, he releases inside me, sinking his teeth into the soft flesh of my neck before collapsing on me in a sweaty heap.

Chapter Twenty-Two
Nate

Peace. Deep. Blissful peace. Four hours of undisturbed sleep with Rachel in my arms has done a world of good, but for the last ten minutes, I've chosen to watch her rest. She wanted to go and sleep with the twins, but I knew I'd never relax with a door between us. Afraid to close my eyes in case Two or Three came sniffing around. So, after cleaning us both up and untying her wrists, I wrapped the duvet around us and pulled her against me.

"What if I shoot you in your sleep?" she'd retorted, ever incapable of backing down.

"Then I'll die happy," was my response. Killing her anger with charm was always the best approach, but I meant it. She's given me her entire body, and

despite all the venom she spits, I suspect I still have her heart.

When you grow up in the world we did, where anything could be taken from you in the blink of an eye, you don't do things by halves. When you give your heart away, you relinquish every tiny piece. Forever.

"Hmmm..." Rachel stirs, her peace disrupted.

"Shush." Raising my hand, I move towards her hair, ready to calm her, but the second I make contact, her body jerks, and she jumps up, gasping for air.

Rachel's eyes dart around the room, trying to place the unfamiliar space. Gripping the sheets with one hand, she presses the other against her frantically beating heart.

"Hey, hey," I soothe, pulling her focus to me. The recognition in her eyes is instant, and she flops back onto the bed after exhaling a deep breath. "You OK?"

"Perfect," she deadpans, turning away from me.

"Not so fast." Rolling her back over, I lean above her, trapping her in place. "What were you dreaming about?"

"Being trapped in a house with three psychos."

Yeah... That would scare most people, but her answer was too quick for it to be real.

"Aren't we past the lies?" It's an honest question, just like I've been truthful in everything I've told her since we got here. She's the one with a heart full of lies—ghosts of beliefs she can't let go of.

"It doesn't matter," she huffs, trying to squirm away.

"I say it does. You were scared." Gripping her chin, I wait until her eyes lock on mine. "Tell me why."

"It's stup—"

"Tell. Me."

Closing her eyes, she tenses her jaw and resigns to her fate. "I fell." Her eyes open, and the light of the moon breaking through the curtains reveals the pain in them. "We were on the balcony... back home. You told me you'd catch me, but... I fell."

Lowering my head, I pause when I'm inches away from her face. "Do you know what I would've done if you had fallen?"

It takes a few moments, but she finally shakes her head.

Of course, she wouldn't know. She's spent all these years telling herself I never loved her. Might as well set the record straight.

Getting even closer, I rest my forehead against hers. "I would've dived to the ground before you. Ready to break your fall."

Sunday
8 am

"Nothing can go wrong," Boss growls down the phone.

"It won't." My words are calmer than my thoughts, but he knows me well enough. No matter how I feel, I'll get this job done as intended without anyone getting hurt.

"How did this get so fucked up?"

161

"You play with fire," I deadpan.

"Yeah."

Neither of us says anything else. This was always a risky job, which is why he didn't agree to it at first, but once he committed… Well, there was no going back for any of us.

"No more comms until you're at base," he states before ending the call.

How this plays out is all on me.

9 am

Three paces around the kitchen as the tension mounts. Grace looks like she's going to vomit, Jeremy—or The Mouse, as we've taken to calling him since he's barely said two words—may soon pass out, and Rachel is like a statue. She watches the clock, speaking only when I talk first or when she needs to deal with the girls.

I spent most of the night and this morning reassuring her that this will all go smoothly, but the closer it gets to her mum arriving, the more scared she's becoming. Dread builds, remorse sitting uncomfortably in my gut. Whatever ground I may have made in my attempts to make Rachel think differently about the past won't matter. Before this day is over, she'll be wishing me dead.

"Shit." Two jumps when Rachel's phone vibrates on the table.

Picking it up, I stare at the message from Rachel's mum before addressing Two and Three. "They're on their way."

"Ivy, Bella."

Rachel eyes me warily when I call her sisters' names. They're sitting on either side of her on the sofa, wrapped around their big sister like they can sense something's coming.

"We've got a game set up for you in your bedroom," I tell them, the only part of my face they see showing nothing but a calm smile.

"Mummy and Daddy will be back soon," Ivy replies, tucking her head closer to Rachel.

I'll take that as a no. Turning my focus to Rachel, who knows exactly what's coming, she jumps into action. "Come on." Sitting up, she pulls the twins with her. "You should tidy the room as well."

"Urrgh…" they both groan in unison.

Smiling, Rachel tickles them. "The sooner it's finished, the sooner you can go home and trash your own bedrooms again." She leads them out of the room, and I follow her, nodding to Three on the way.

"Kitchen," I hear him say to Grace and Jeremy as we ascend the stairs.

Rachel walks slowly, her hands flexing as she silently manages her fear, but there's no hint of it in her voice when she ushers the twins into the room.

"What's the game?" Bella asks, her tone leaving no doubt that I've outstayed my welcome.

Still, I keep the smile plastered on my face. "Tidy up, like your sister told you, then hide so you can surprise your parents."

At that last part, a glimmer of their mischievous nature shines. "Remember to be quiet," I add. "Or you'll be stinky losers."

Leaving them giggling, I grip Rachel's arm and pull her away. "Aren't I staying with them?" she asks, panic in her voice, even though she's still keeping it low.

"No." I've been dreading this moment ever since I decided to do it. She's going to be furious, but it's for the best. Locking the door as we leave, I walk her towards the room we've spent so much time together in.

"Why?"

Because I can't trust you not to break the door down when you hear your mum. "It's for the best. Sit down and put your hands behind your back."

"Nate wh—"

"That's exactly why I have to do this," I seethe quietly against her ear. She'll blow our cover. She won't be able to help it, and if Two and Three discover the truth, this house will be covered in the blood of innocents. "Sit down. Be quiet, and I promise you everything will be OK."

Glancing at the clock, we have twenty-five minutes left. I can't afford for her to fight me, but thankfully, she doesn't. Kneeling, Rachel puts her hands behind her back, and I fix them together with cable ties. She says nothing but flinches when I tear a strip off the roll of gaffer tape.

"No way!"

"Press your lips together," I order calmly.

"I said no!" She attempts to climb to her knees, but I force her to the floor as she kicks against me.

Legs on either side of her, thankful that her hands are secured, I wrap one arm around her neck and press her mouth shut before quickly slapping the tape over it. Her screams are silenced, but her legs are still a problem.

Keeping as much weight on her as I can, I twist my body so I can grab her legs. Using my size to my advantage, I shuffle lower until I sit on her shins, preventing her feet from flying at my face. Wrapping a cable tie around each ankle, I secure them together with another. It's not enough. She'll still be able to drag herself across the floor and slam her feet against the door. Even if she can't break it, the noise will be too distracting for everyone.

Standing, I grab the duvet, take it into the bathroom and lay it in the bathtub. Next, I scoop Rachel up from the floor—her attempts to slam her head into my back do nothing to deter me. Sweat pools at the base of my spine, and my heart hammers at a mile a minute. Every second spent sorting Rachel out brings us closer to the arrival of her mum and stepdad, and I must be at that front door when that happens.

Placing her in the bath as gently as her thrashing will allow, I lay her on the side and secure her feet to the taps. She's going nowhere, and while it's not the best setup, it's the comfiest I can make her.

"Mmmmmmmh," Rachel screams against the tape, and I look at her face for the first time since restraining her. Her hair sticks to the tears streaming *along her cheeks. She's bright red, panting, desperate, her eyes pleading with me.*

Don't break Nate.

Leaving her, I go to the bedroom and lock the door, glancing at the clock as I do. Fifteen minutes... how is time moving so fast?

Safe—alone—I go back to the ensuite and remove my mask. Gripping her head in both hands, I get as close as I dare. "I had to do this. And you have to trust me." With that, I press my lips to her forehead and quickly pull away. Taking one last look, I push her hair away from her face and behind her ears, replace my mask, and walk away.

Chapter Twenty-Three
Nate

The security system alerts us to the front gate opening. Johnson doesn't need to call—he has the code.

"Oh God," Grace gasps, causing Three to press the barrel of the gun against her head.

My glare lands on him, and he eases off. "No need for that." We have one minute before they pull up, and the doubts are swirling. I need them both in the house for this to work, and that part isn't in my hands.

Keeping people calm is within my power, though. "Grace…" Pausing, I wait until she focuses on me. The woman's going to need a stiff drink after this. "We've not hurt anyone this whole time we've been here, and we don't plan for that to change."

"The girls—"

"Are pissed off but fine."

"Ra-Rachel," she whispers.

"Even more pissed off, but also fine," I assure her with a smile. "They're out of the way." Pulling the two keys from my pocket, I ensure she sees them before I put them back. "And I'll return them to you once we're done."

Gravel crunches as the tyres roll across it, and I rush to the front door, taking my place to the side. Blood rushes against my ears as my heart races, the finale upon us. It's hard to listen to anything else, but

I don't need to hear their footsteps to know I have seconds until the door opens.

Everything happens in slow motion, like the Devil is giving me the time I need to get this right. The key scrapes against metal, the lock twists, the handle turns, and the door opens. Three... two... one.

Trish. My left arm is around her neck in an instant, my hand crushing her mouth closed. My right arm, now light as a feather, brings the gun up, holding it in front of her eyes so she can see the severity of the situation before I press it against the side of her head.

The shock keeps her silent long enough for Johnson to enter. He clears the door; I slam it shut. The man of the hour spins around, and although he sees the masked man holding a gun to his wife's head, it takes him a few seconds to process, and I use that to my advantage.

"You do everything I say or lose your entire family today. Understand?"

Slowly, he raises his hands, his car keys dropping to the floor. His pale blue eyes widen, his fresh-from-holiday tan fades, and his swallow echoes around the hallway. "L-l-let's just keep calm," he stutters.

"My thoughts exactly." Removing the gun from Trish's head, I use it to gesture towards the kitchen. "Keep those hands where I can see them, walk to the kitchen, and sit on the chair closest to the laptop."

"Please don't hurt her," he whispers, all choked up as he follows my command.

"Whether people get hurt or not is down to you."

Johnson enters the kitchen and then stops, but only for a moment before he takes his seat. He looks up at me like a lost child waiting for his next instruction.

Saying nothing, I guide Trish to her seat on the other side. "Sit," I order, removing my hand from her mouth.

"Where are my girls?" she demands, the second she has the chance.

"Safe."

"What do you want?" she screeches, acting way more panicked than I thought her capable. The Trish, I remember, was all business.

"Glad you asked—"

"Have you hurt—"

The barrel of my gun pressing against her skull cuts her off. "Interrupt again, and Jeremy will pay the price. After that, it'll be Grace, and after that, I'll be popping upstairs to play Eeny Meeny Miney Moe. Got it?"

Trish nods vigorously just as the girls begin banging on their bedroom door. Johnson starts to rise from his chair but quickly thinks better of it.

"Let's get this done, One," Three barks, his agitation growing.

"Johnson. What does the note on the laptop say?"

Eyes wide, he stares at the scrap of paper I placed there. "Three million pounds."

"That's right. Now, turn it over."

Fumbling, his fingers weak, he turns it over and slams his hand over his mouth, holding in the cry that almost escapes when he sees the details for a bank account that's not supposed to exist.

"You're going to open that account, and then hand me that laptop. By the end of all this, you'll be three million lighter, but you'll get to keep your family intact."

"Sounds like a fair deal to me," Two quips, a cruel grin on his face.

"We-we don't have that money," Trish protests.

"You're not supposed to, no. And yet, you do. Tick tock, Johnson, your little girls are getting impatient, and so am I," I warn. I'm over this job and desperate to get the fuck out of here.

"Then you'll leave?" Johnson asks, fingers shaking as he types his password.

"Yes. We'll leave, but if you make any attempt to reverse the transaction, we'll come back to wipe you fucking out. All of you."

"Please, son," Jeremy begs. "Please… I just want this to be over."

"Here." Johnson slides the laptop to me.

"Two," I order, and he steps around the table to point his gun at Johnson's head as I leave Trish and take the laptop to the worktop. Blowing out a whistle, I can't help but laugh when I see the total: just shy of nine million pounds. They'll make back what we take in interest in no time.

"Take the lot," Three calls, and I pin him in place with a glare.

"We take what was agreed and not a penny more."

Not allowing anyone else to distract me, I transfer the money to an account I've memorised, then go into Johnson's profile and change the contact email address to a new one I've created. My phone pings almost instantly, and I verify the request before changing the password. It doesn't make it impossible for him to get back in, but it will take time, and I'll know when he tries.

Closing the laptop, I face them all and smile. "Job done." Walking back to the table, I place my free hand on Trish's shoulder. "Thank you for making good choices. You can return to your unscrupulous lives and pretend this never happened."

"You won't get away with this," Trish snaps, the only person here with a pair of balls. "We'll call the po—"

"No, Trish," Johnson interrupts, his voice thick with guilt. "No police."

Ding fucking dong.

Trish's shoulders rise and fall at speed, but I ignore it—her rage isn't for me.

"Grace. Jeremy. Thank you for your hospitality. Trish… your daughters are lovely, a real credit to you." Nodding to Two and Three, they step away, guns aimed at their targets as they move towards the door that leads to the garage where our car's been parked this whole time.

Once they're out of sight, I follow them, facing the table as I edge backwards. Grinning, I can't help myself as I add, "Especially Rachel."

Trish's gaze turns from her husband to me, her face covered in red splotches as she watches me lick my lips. "I enjoyed Rachel very much."

"Fuck you," she spits out, barely a whisper as she practically convulses. "Fuck. You!" she screeches, tears streaming down her cheeks. I must admit, the pleasure her anger gives me will keep me going for quite some time.

Blowing her a kiss, I step over the threshold to the garage. "Grace. The keys you need will be on the paint shelf. Wait until we're gone to retrieve them."

After one last glance at the ceiling, as if somehow I'll be able to see Rachel through the floorboard and plaster, I slam the door shut and jump into the driver's seat.

"Let's fucking go," Three shouts from the passenger seat.

Starting the car, I roll slowly down the driveway, not bringing any attention to us by driving like a twat. Three opens the window, types in the code, and the gates slowly open, aiding our escape. I keep my eyes straight ahead because there's no looking back now. No looking back, no going back. My heart sinks as I drive away, putting more distance between me and Rachel, but there's a spark of hope because I know I've not seen the last of her.

Oh, no. Tony will be hearing from her very soon.

Chapter Twenty-Four
Rachel

The girls banging on their door echoes the hammering of my heart, the blood rocketing against my ears. My ankles ache from my failed attempts to free them. Mum should be here by now... she must be. I have no idea how long I've been in this bath, and other than the girls, I've heard nothing else over the pounding in my head.

It will be fine. It will. Dad's in charge, and Nate promised. He promised it would be fine. Clinging to his words, his sincerity, I repeat them like a mantra because it's all I've got. If I let the doubt creep in, then I have to accept that I might lose someone I love today, and I can't do that. Thoughts have power. They send a message to the universe, tempting it to make them true, and that can't happen.

My dress sticks to my back as panic floods through me. The girls keep banging, reminding me they're still alive, so I hold on to that as I pull the air through my nostrils. Then I stop. Everything stops when I hear footsteps running up the stairs. As the fear takes hold, the blood pulses even louder, preventing my attempts to get more details. Screams. The girls definitely just screamed, and the sound has me pulling at the restraints again.

The footsteps get louder—another latch opening. He lied... they're coming for me. The door flies open, crashing against the wall, and a guttural scream reverberates through my skull.

"Oh my God, oh my God," Mum gasps, dropping to her knees. She cups my face. "Rachel... Oh God. Stop!" she shrieks, facing the door. "Don't let them in here! Get me some fucking scissors!"

The clock on my phone tells me I've been in the bath for an hour. This time, it's full of water and in my flat.

The bubbles have all disappeared, and I've had to add extra warm water twice. As soon as Mum freed me from my restraints, she sat me on the bed in the girls' room while she gathered all their belongings together. Once packed, she took my hand and guided me downstairs, dropped the bags by the feet of my crying sisters, stood listening to the shouting in the kitchen, grabbed my bag and marched us all to my car.

It's still a blur, but I remember Johnson running after us and Mum refusing to speak. He chanced a glance at me just once, and the guilt in his face almost crippled me, reminding me that I'm supposed to be a victim. Technically, I am, yet it feels like a lie.

Mum drove us all back to mine, put the girls in front of the TV, and ran me a bath. She's been in to give me a cup of tea, but it's sitting cold on the side, untouched because all I can do is stare at my phone and wait. Wait for either Dad to call me or for me to be left alone so I can call him.

"Can I come in?" Mum opens the door, so I pull my knees up to my chest. It makes me look vulnerable—I see it in her eyes. Another lie. I only did it because the bubbles are gone.

"Sweetheart... what do you need from me?"

To leave me alone. "I don't know."

"Do you..." Pausing, she clears her throat. "Do you need to see a doctor?"

Shaking my head, I remember that the most important thing I need to do is take my pill and glance at my bathroom cabinet. "No."

"Rach—"

"Can you pass me my towel, please?" How can I have this conversation with her? How can I tell her that while I wasn't given much of a choice, I don't feel like I was raped? That I never felt scared because I knew who it was, and I loved every sinful second of it?

"What do you need?" Mum presses, holding the towel up so I can climb out.

Another question I can't answer. What I want is to be alone so I can yell at my dad for causing all this. "We can't tell the police." Wrapping the towel around me, I wait for her to protest, to scream that it doesn't matter what happens to Johnson, but she doesn't.

"Do you want to?" she asks, her voice shaking. It's not surprising; she could lose her husband, and the twins will lose their father. That's not what I want. I also don't want Dad locked up again because that will prevent me from killing him.

"No. I just want some space."

"Rach… I can arrange for you to speak to someone. What you've been through—"

"What? What do you think I've been through?" Go on. Say the word.

"That man… he—" She looks down, unable to say it, before staring me in the eyes, her face set firm. "Just give me five fucking minutes in a room with him. I'll—"

"Mummy…"

Mum runs her hands down her face, erasing the hate and replacing it with a smile as she turns around.

"When can we go home?" Ivy asks.

"Now," I respond before Mum can. "You can all go home now."

Mum left after much protesting almost thirty minutes ago, and as desperate as I was for this moment to come, now, I can't face it. Fuck it! It needs to be done. Sucking in as much air as possible, I find his contact in my phone and hit dial. My hands shake. For years, I've told myself I didn't matter to my dad, but I never truly let it sink in. My stubborn mind kept reinforcing it, but my heart always held hope. Then Nate… he fuelled the fire, and as much as my heart wants to believe him, my brain is guarded. This conversation will determine which is right—my head or my heart, and that's terrifying.

"Hello, Flower." Dad's deep voice sends warmth to my ear, but his calm tone has me raging. "I've been expecting you."

"I bet you fucking have," I spit back. Where do I start? "Give me one reason why I shouldn't land you in it?"

"I can give you plenty." He sounds calm, but I hear the tell-tale sign of him smoking a cigarette. "But is that really what you want to ask me?"

"Why? That's what I want to ask. Why and how could you do this to her?"

"It's complic—"

"No. No. It's really fucking simple. You went after your ex… the woman you used to love, the mother of your only child."

"I can't give you the answers you want… not now. I'm gonna come see you."

"The fuck are you coming anywhere near me!"

"When the dust settles," he continues, as if I didn't speak. "I'll put this right, but I need you to give it some time so that—"

"Two and Three go back to wherever they came from?" This time, answer for him.

"Yes. When it's safe for you, then—"

The laugh escapes before I even feel it coming. "Safe? Like I've just been safe for the last two days?"

"Baby, baby, baby…" he exhales like the weight of the world is on his shoulders. "You were never meant to be involved."

"I feel like I've heard that once or twice from your golden boy Nate." As soon as his name leaves my mouth, the flames in me burn brighter. Dad's not going to give me what I need right now, and all it's doing is fuelling my need to destroy, and I have the perfect target.

"Although he seemed to enjoy me being there… multiple times."

Silence.

"But you already knew that… didn't you?" You told him to.

"I can't make you understand right no—"

"He came in my mouth."

The air whooshes out of him straight into the phone, and I don't care how uncomfortable this makes him feel.

"But it's OK because he was proving a point, right? Just like he was proving a point when he came inside my cunt."

"Can we not?"

"Not sure the arse fucking session was nec—"

"Stop!" Raising his voice for the first time, I know my words have had the desired effect. "I can't do this right now. We will," he adds, sensing my objection. "Rach… You need to know that I would burn alive any man who hurt you."

"Except Nate." Swallowing the pain this statement digs up—the day I realised I was second best, I push on. "Will Nate pay for touching me?"

"I love you," he confesses, stunning me. I can't remember when I last heard him say that. I haven't given him the chance in years, just in case the opportunity presented itself and he chose not to take it. "I will fix this. I promise."

"But only when you're ready," I add bitterly.

"No. Only when it's safe."

Chapter Twenty-Five
Rachel

"I can't take this anymore."

My eyes rise lazily towards my office door. Kim, my boss, stands staring at me with her arms across her chest. It's been a week and a half since I called in sick on Monday morning. A fake stomach bug bought me a week off work and kept Tasha at bay. As much as I needed her light, I couldn't risk her seeing through the lies. For the entire time, I stayed in my flat, waiting for a call that never came.

I never made a call either. It was up to Dad to call me. Nate's job to reach out and grovel at my feet. Neither happened, and I went from the high of believing they were doing what was best for me to the low, where their professions of love... of always caring for me were just words used to shut me up.

Dad may have left me hanging, but Johnson didn't. I'm now two hundred thousand pounds richer thanks to the trauma he thinks he's inflicted on me. He wasn't daft enough to suggest he was buying my silence—I'm supposed to use it to get therapy. To make peace with what happened since I can't seek justice via the courts.

He stumbled all over himself, apologising— grovelling. At least he had the sense not to ask me to help him with Mum, who's currently living with the girls at Grandma's in Long Eaton, with no intention of going back to him.

"Rachel?" Kim says, when I don't respond straight away. "Pack up your things."

"What?" I jump up, fearing the worst. I've not exactly been with it for the few days I've been here.

"You have nineteen days' worth of holiday left to take." She steps forward. "You're taking them now."

"I've just had a week off," I protest. The last thing I need is more time to myself.

"Ill, Rachel. Being sick isn't a holiday." Reaching my desk, she takes the seat opposite me. "You're a talent. I want you to grow with this business, but I'm also willing to say goodbye if this isn't the right fit."

"Have I done something wrong?"

"No. But you're not happy," she smiles. "I can't put my finger on it… You're great at your job, but I've realised you're on autopilot."

"I-I.."

"It's not an insult, and you're not in trouble. I would hate to see you burn out, or worse… just. I don't know… fade out."

Fade out. Her words take me back to Nate, to that room where he accused me of living a lie. Of hiding who I am.

"Take this time to think about where you want to be." Rising, she smiles. "Your job will be waiting for you if you still want it."

One more street to go, and I can crawl into my flat. After my day finished earlier than expected, I opted for a spot of retail therapy, courtesy of my lovely new bank balance. It offered a temporary distraction, but now my arms feel as full as my head, as heavy as my heart.

It's getting dark, but the streets are quiet, and most people have yet to finish their day. How the hell am I going to figure out my life in nineteen days?

"Excuse me." A man in all black stands next to his van, map in hand, his face hidden by his cap. "I'm trying to figure out this one-way system."

Try upgrading to a sat nav. Standing a few metres away from him, I opt for politeness. "Where are you going?"

Dropping his map through the passenger seat window, he slides the side door wide open, eyes on me. *Fuck.* Every tiny hair on my body stands to attention as fear weaves through my senses and makes roots in my gut. Stepping back, I try to formulate a plan. My hands are full of shopping bags, but they're all clothes, nothing that would do any damage, no matter how hard I swung them at him.

"Probably straight to hell," the man says, letting his real accent slip through. It's still one I can't place, but I know who it belongs to.

"Two," I gasp, the word sticking in my throat. Dropping my bags, I spin around only to slam straight into another body. Arms grip my sides, holding me in place while my legs are swept out from under me, and a rag covered in a blinding substance steals my breath.

"But you're coming with us," the menacing voice whispers against my ear as I turn weightless and float away into nothing.

"Wakey, wakey."

The voice sounds far away, like a dream. My eyes feel too heavy to open, my throat too dry to speak, but I'm cold. That's what brings me around: my prickling skin, the pain in my wrists, the pressure at my knees.

Pieces of a puzzle start to fit together. A van, a man. "Agh!" *A clammy palm makes contact with my cheek, slamming my head to the side and forcing my eyes wide open. Blinking, I try to focus on the scene. I'm on the floor, I can't move my hands, and as my heart regains its ability to beat, I realise I'm completely naked.*

"Here she is... almost missed all the fun."

Pulling my heavy head back to the centre, I focus on the man in front of me. Though I never saw his face, I remember the smile. It always held a threat, and never more so than now. Swallowing, I force my eyes to lift higher to see another unwelcome face peering over me—Three. The reason I can't move my arms.

Closing my eyes, I suck in as much air as possible. A myriad of emotions fly at me: betrayal, fear, revulsion, embarrassment. Yet, lying here completely naked, it's rage that hits me the hardest. If I'm to die, I'll do it angry. Not scared. Strong, not weak. Alone, but one hundred per cent me.

Opening my eyes, I glare at Two. "Now I know why you wore masks."

Two bursts out laughing, his nails sinking into my knees as he spreads them wider. "This is going to be fun." Thinking I'm One's little submissive, he releases my right leg to undo his zip, and I take the moment to show my teeth.

My knee rises in the air so fast he barely sees it happen, and I slam the heel of my foot straight into his nose. The bone crunches, blood gushes and Two staggers back, clutching his face.

Hope spikes, but only for a second.

"Bitch!" Three's fist slams straight into my gut, forcing all the air out of my body, the pain causing vomit to burn my throat. Twisting to the side, I try to gasp for air, but Three's foot connecting with my back sends me flying, the ground grazing my hip as it drags across the floor.

"We were going to be nice," Three growls. "Make it fun." Looming over me, he kicks me onto my back, his spit landing on my face. "Now you'll bleed like the others. They'll never find all the pieces of you."

"You-you won't get away with this," I gasp, as he drags me across the ground by my feet. "He'll know it was you."

Three laughs, "Nobody gives a fuck about you."

"Tony does," I splutter, and the reaction is instant.

Three drops my feet to the ground, a flicker of fear in his eyes. "And who the fuck is Tony to you?"

A wave of air slams over my skin, and on instinct, I roll into the fetal position. "Rachel," a panicked voice cries against my ear as I'm again made weightless. "Quick, get this on her."

Warmth, a different voice, familiar but unexpected. "Open your eyes."

The voice is friendly, so I do as he asks. "Benny," I smile.

"Oh, thank fuck," he chokes, pulling me closer. "I thought you were fucking gone."

Slowly, my senses kick in. First, I notice the large coat draped over me, then the other people around me—men. Dad's men. Like a rogue wave crashing against a cliff, I come back to reality with a crash.

"Who's Tony?" A voice booms, and I spin to face it. "I'm her fucking dad!" Holding Three by his throat, Dad rains blows against his face, without pause or mercy, as Three slips into oblivion.

Mesmerised, I watch until a guttural scream has my head spinning to my right. Nate... he came for me. Sitting on top of a man with no face left to identify him, Nate roars and spits as he continues to beat the bloodied mess that's no longer breathing.

"Stop." Jack steps up behind Nate, wraps his arms around him and stills his onslaught. "He's done."

"Rachel." Dad reaches out to me, but stops when my eyes land on his blood-covered hands. "What did I say I'd do? Do you remember… when we spoke? What did I say?"

You love me, is the first thing that springs to mind because I believe it now, but that's not the answer he wants. Looking past him, I see Three on the floor. He's barely conscious, but he's still breathing. He doesn't deserve to be.

"They've done this before," I say, more to myself than anyone. Resolute, I focus on my dad, a mix of rage, fear and love written all over his face. "Burn him alive."

Chapter Twenty-Six
Rachel

Dad had me carried out before he set Three alight, but I heard the flames take hold. Benny and a few others brought me to Dad's house and wrapped me in blankets. This is where I've stayed since. People keep talking, but not to me. It's like murmurs as they speak on phones and share instructions as they go about cleaning up this mess. Mess... two dead bodies.

"Oh, sweetheart."

Shocked, I remain motionless as Mum charges through the door, jumps on the sofa and wraps herself around me. "How are you here?" I mumble against her hair.

"Dad called."

"But..." How long have I been here?

"I'm here now. You're safe. That's all that matters." Mum bursts into tears, and I try to free my arms so I can hug her back. Releasing me, she looks me in the eyes as her fear turns to guilt. "This is all my fault."

"Trish." Dad enters the room, kneels at my feet, and picks up the bag Mum dropped on the floor. "Let her get dressed first."

Dad leaves the room, and Mum turns away, giving me some privacy. The numbness that's engulfed me for the last—what, a few hours?—leaves my body, pins and needles taking its place as I pull items of clothing from the bag. Once dressed, I wrap the blanket around me, more for safety than warmth. "Why do I feel like the world is about to implode on me?"

A sob rips through Mum's body, and she doubles over. Usually, I'd rush to comfort her, but my instincts keep me firmly in place. Dad returns and hands me a glass, and I watch Mum cry, clutching her sides. The bourbon slides down my throat, my pulse quickens and my patience crumbles.

"I think it's time for an explanation. I don't care which one of you gives it to me, but you'd better hurry the fuck up."

Wiping her eyes, Mum turns to face me. She steps closer, but I hold up my hand, warning her to keep away. "Why is this your fault?"

Swallowing deeply, she sucks in a breath. "Because it is," she exhales. "This whole thing was my idea."

Taking another sip, I inhale deeply, the slight tilt of my head her cue to continue.

"Johnson isn't who I thought he was," she sniffs, regaining some control. "When I found out about the other women, I told him I wanted a divorce."

Closing my eyes, I shake my head, this story is already shit, and it's only the beginning.

"He laughed in my face. Told me I'd get nothing, but I didn't care. All I wanted was my girls. So... so the fucking prick told me that I'd never be able to afford the type of lawyers needed to clear my name after he painted me as an unfit mother."

Gulping her drink, she settles in the seat opposite me. "I did leave him... for a bit, and during that time, he gave me a taste of what was to come."

"So, you went back."

"For my girls, not for him. But..." she exhales, shakily. "I wasn't going to let him win. He'd opened my eyes to who he was, so I kept them open. I listened, too. That's how I discovered the truth about the bank accounts he managed for his parents."

Rising, she comes to sit next to me. "I just needed to have something over him."

"So you faked a fucking robbery?"

"It was only going to be three hours. That's all. I knew Nate would keep the girls safe. It was just going to be a fun game they'd soon forget." Forcing a bitter laugh, she gulps down the rest of her drink. "Do you want to know why our holiday was extended? Why it all went to shit? He was fucking the receptionist and wanted to have her a few more times before we left."

My stomach lurches when I picture the scene—everything Mum had to endure, but my sympathy only stretches so far. "Why didn't you call it off?"

"My bags were already packed when Johnson announced we were staying, and your Dad cut off communication, I—"

"And you just agreed to this shit show?" I scoff, facing Dad.

He shakes his head. "Not at first."

"I just needed to have the power over him, Rachel," she attempts to justify. "Taking the money didn't matter, it was the leverage I wanted, and—"

"And you got it."

"Rachel..." She tries to touch me, but I yank my arm away. "I was supposed to get there three hours after it started; they'd take the money and go, and I could use the severity of the situation and their tax evasion to get him to agree to giving me full custody."

Placing my head in my hands, I take in a few deep breaths, trying to let this whole new level of fucked-upness sink in.

"Rach—"

"No." Sitting up straight, I look Mum in the eye. "I can get this. It's fucked up, but I can understand that you felt helpless... I can. But Mum... I was nearly—"

"Give me the room, Trish," Dad interrupts, and Mum leaves—too defeated, too guilty to argue.

Once she's gone, Dad refills my glass and kneels before me. "I have no right to ask for your forgiveness. Neither of us does." Nodding, he grinds his teeth. "We *fucked up big time, and it almost cost me the thing that matters most to me in this world."*

Lowering my gaze, I wipe away a rogue tear and take another sip of my drink.

"I had no doubt Nate would keep you safe—I know what you think," he adds when I roll my eyes. "Yes, Nate means a lot to me, but I also knew I could trust him with those girls… with you."

Staring at him, my face void of emotion because I have no idea which one to let take hold, I force out the words, "You. Told. Him. To. Fuck. Me."

Dragging his hands down his face, he exhales a deep sigh. "You don't know how my world works."

"BECAUSE YOU NEVER WANTED TO BE AROUND ME!" My glass smashes against the wall before I realise I threw it, and Dad jumps up, holding my hands in place.

"I wanted you!" he yells back. "More than anything, sweetheart. I wanted you in my life."

"You didn't fight for me," I sob, my fifteen-year-old broken-hearted self, climbing to the surface—the trauma of the night paling in comparison to the rejection of my childhood. Dad just killed a man for hurting me—that ought to be enough—but these wounds run deep.

"He did," Mum says, appearing next to me again. "When we left London, he came to drag you back. But—"

"She made me see what was right for you," Dad says, calmer now.

"Because I had sex with Nate?" The secret flows out of me, along with the tears.

"No," Dad says, a tick appearing in his jaw. "I didn't know about that until you were eighteen. When I thought I'd be welcoming you home." Shaking his head, he releases my hands and gives me his glass since mine is in pieces. "The hold you two had over each other was obvious—everyone could see it, even after all that time apart. Your Mum's words made more sense to me then. And I just knew that if you stayed—"

"You'd end up like me," Mum interrupts. "It broke my heart when your Dad went to jail, and I sent him packing when he came out so that I didn't have to feel that way again."

Dad looks down, hiding his feelings. All this time, I thought she had fallen out of love with him. Turns out she was just protecting herself.

The cogs of my life fall into place, the decisions people made with my best intentions at heart. "This is all very lovely… but you both forgot one thing." They stare at me intently, nothing but love in their eyes. "You forgot to ask me what I wanted."

"What do you want, Rach?" Dad asks.

You're dead on the inside.

You're on autopilot.

The secret I've kept from myself. "That's the problem, Dad. I don't know."

Chapter Twenty-Seven
Rachel

Waking with a start, I toss the covers off me and sit bolt upright, panting. My parents and I talked a lot last night, until too many tears had been shed and I couldn't keep my eyes open. Maybe it was a delay tactic on my part, or perhaps settling the past mattered most, but once the lights were out, my mind was plagued by Two and Three—Vic and Jonno... it seems weird giving them actual names. Whether I was asleep or awake, I played out what happened on a loop—their hands holding me down, spreading me wide, the fact that I was seconds away from being raped and horrifically murdered.

They're dead. They're dead. They're dead.

They died, not me, because Dad and Nate ended them. Nate's blood-covered fists, the tortured expression haunts me still. Dad told me Nate's the reason they found me in time. They almost didn't, but I can't dwell on that. It seems Nate didn't trust that Vic and Jonno would just walk away after getting paid, and they 'put eyes on them' as Dad called it. The shit-eating-cum-stained-arsehole-worthless cunts ditched the van on the way to Nottingham and Nate had to use every trick he knew and call in every outstanding favour Dad was owed to find them. If they hadn't brought me back to London—more familiar territory for them, my story would've ended differently.

"Fuck this." Forcing myself up, I switch on the light, taking in the room Dad decorated for me years ago. He never changed it, keeping it for me in case I needed or wanted it. Despite what happened last night, I feel so much lighter. The baggage I've been carrying all these years is finally being checked in to where it belongs—the bin—because what I always believed was utter crap.

Grabbing the bag Mum brought for me, I find enough clothes to last a few days, so I take it with me to the bathroom and run a hot shower. Smothering a fresh sponge with soap, I scrub myself free of the memory of last night until my whole body stings as much as the grazes down my side. It feels good, like I've physically eradicated them from me. My head will take more time, but thankfully, that's something I have.

Hushed voices fill the living room as I walk down the stairs, so I keep my steps light to help me hear. We're done with secrets. Pressing my ear to the door, my heart sinks as I immediately get the gist of Dad's words: "He's blaming himself... I'll come and get him."

Nate. Dad jumps out of his skin when I barge through the door. "Where is he?"

"Rach..." Dad walks up to me, resting his hands on my shoulders. "It's nothing for you to worry about."

"It is," I argue. Nate has always been mine to worry about.

Dad looks in my eyes and grins, no doubt recognising the expression he's seen so many times in Mum, which means there's no chance in hell that I'm backing down. "He's down the local."

Glancing at the clock for the first time today, I realise it's already 12:15. Nate must've arrived as soon as it opened. Looking back at Dad, I force a swallow, the thought of leaving his side suddenly grounding me.

Dad shakes his head and walks to the door, knowing me better than I ever thought possible. "We best get going then."

We enter the already heaving pub, a familiar face coming to greet us. "Benny..." Reaching forward, I wrap my arms around the beast of a man, pushing the fact that he saw me completely naked last night from my mind—I doubt he even looked.

"Here she is." He squeezes me tightly. "You gave us all a fucking fright."

"Just keeping you on your toes," I smile, remembering all the times Benny and my Dad's closest men—friends, no... family—would spend time playing with me, getting me gifts, making me feel completely safe. Stupid how I got so blinded by grief that I let myself forget.

Stepping back, I glance around the room, but Benny turns me, pointing me in the direction I need to go. My feet move the second my eyes land on a man hunched over the bar wearing grey sweatpants and a hoodie to match. Claiming the seat next to him without him noticing, I grab his glass and smell the clear liquid he's drowning himself in.

"Vodka," I snort, my voice laced with disgust.

Nate's eyes widen in recognition, but it only takes a second for them to fill with shame.

"You're not your mother." *You're not going to destroy yourself like she did.*

Realising a stiff drink is probably what I need right now, I bring the glass back to my mouth, only for it to be snatched from my hand. "Neither are you," Nate grits out, knocking the glass away from us both.

"What can I get you?" the barman asks, eyes locked on me as he nervously avoids making any contact with Nate.

"Anything from the top shelf, please." Tilting my head towards Nate, I add, "And he's done for the day."

Nate remains silent, but I feel his eyes burning into me.

"Is that your call?" the barman asks, risking a glance at Nate.

It's been a long time since I've used Dad's name to my advantage, and I know this guy is just trying to stay in Nate's good books, but I don't have time for niceties.

Spinning on my chair, I locate Dad, who's watching the scene, and turn back to face the barman. "Yes, it is. And if you have a problem with that, you can take it up with my dad."

Following where my gaze landed, the barman blows a low whistle and says nothing more, and thirty seconds later, he hands me a large glass of Baileys. Not what I expected. Though it was from the top shelf. I haven't eaten, so let's call it brunch.

Nate no longer looks at me, his eyes focused on the beermat he's picking at.

"I told myself that when I saw you again, I'd kick you in the balls so hard you'd impregnate your tonsils."

Nate's lips pull into a slight grin—I'll take it. "What changed?" he asks, his voice slurring.

Turning to face him, I twist him around, so he has to look at me. "Seems a bit of a bitch thing to do to someone who saved my life."

Nate pulls away, shaking his head vehemently. "I should've never sent him to get your bag."

For a moment, I have no idea what he means, but then I go back to that first night when Two fetched my bag from the car. Nate had kept it hidden in a wardrobe, but Two must've looked at my driving licence. That's how they knew where to find me.

"You're not to blame for what happened. Mum told me everything and you—"

"Fucked up," he interrupts.

"You saved me."

Nate returns to staring at his hands, and I sip my drink. It's going straight to my head, but I need the buzz. "Can I ask you something?"

Silence.

It wasn't a 'no'. Keeping my voice low, I continue, "Why did you kill him?"

Exhaling a deep breath, Nate turns to face me. "Isn't that obvious?"

"No," I blurt out, causing a few people to stare. Ignoring them, I keep pressing him. "You completely lost it... It was like you switched something off, and I need to know..." Inhaling more air, I take another drink and rip the plaster off. "Did you do it out of duty to my dad or out of..." I stop, unable to say the word. "Or was it because of me?"

At the mention of Dad, Nate looks over in his direction, a vacant expression on his face. "I'd do anything that man asked of me."

Rejection never stops stinging, and it's my turn to focus on anything but him.

"But in that moment..." Nate continues. "If he had told me to stop. To stop hitting him, to walk away, to let him live... I wouldn't have listened."

Slowly, I lift my head and let my eyes land on Nate's.

"I didn't stop until someone made me because all I could think about was destroying him. All I could see was you dead on the ground, bloody and broken, and I wanted to cause as much damage as possible."

Resting my hands on his, I bring him back to the room. "That didn't happen."

Raising his hand, he brushes his finger gently across the bruise forming on my cheek. "This was enough. They never should've got within spitting distance."

Closing my eyes, I lean into his touch, but it's gone too soon, leaving me empty and wanting. I had no plan when I came here. Mum and Dad gave me their truths last night, but Nate gave me his weeks ago—in a roundabout way. All I know is that my anger dissolved when he finally fought for me.

Sighing, I turn back to the bar and sip my drink.

"Are you OK?" Nate asks, breaking the silence.

"No." Facing him, I give him a small smile. "But I will be."

We sit in silence for a few more minutes, me drinking, him lost in thought. "What happens next, Rach?"

Ah... the famous question—what do I want?

Exhaling a laugh that almost gets stuck in my throat, I look him in the eyes. "I don't know yet, but I can't go back to how things were before."

"Before..." Nate clears his throat. "As in when you were in London. With me?"

"No," I reply honestly. "Before life woke me up rather aggressively."

"Rach—"

"Look, all I know for certain is that things have changed," I interrupt. "I've changed, or maybe I've reverted to who I always was, but in an older, wiser, and more jaded way."

Nate smiles—innocent and hopeful, making what I need to do next even harder.

"People have made choices for me my whole life, and that stops."

Nate's smile fades, but I push on. "Today, right here, that stops. I have about three weeks to figure out what's right for me, and I need to do it alone."

Throwing the remains of my drink down my throat, I lick my lips, take a deep breath, wrap my arms around Nate's neck and pull him in for a kiss. Vodka mixes with Bailey's—bittersweet—as love mixes with fear, pain with hope, longing with regret. A million emotions pour into a three-second kiss that leaves us both breathless.

Pulling back slightly, Nate rests his forehead against mine. "What was that for?"

"Saving my life." Rising from my chair, I gesture to Dad that I'm ready to leave, and he quickly gets to his feet. He's two strides from me when I turn around and march back to Nate, who, this time, is ready.

Sensing my need, he pulls me against him as soon as I'm in reach, and our lips crash together. We're completely in sync, our tongues dancing, fighting to take the lead, until Dad clears his throat behind me.

Laughing, I pull away and catch my breath, our foreheads meeting again.

"What was that one for?" Nate asks, a smile in his voice.

"I'm not sure... but I think it might be a placeholder."

"A placeholder?" Nate laughs. Leaning back, he regains his composure and locks his gaze on mine. "I'll take that. For now."

Epilogue
Rachel

"I can't tell you how good it is to have you back," Kim beams, the evening light illuminating her face as she stands by the window.

"I can't tell you how good it is to be back." After three weeks of soul searching and occasionally freaking out, my nightmares have faded away, and I'm finally where I'm meant to be.

Joining her at the window, I gaze out at the streets below filled with people speed-walking down the pavement, dodging tourists and cyclists.

"You made the right decision. I've never seen you look so—"

"Me?"

"Exactly." She nods proudly. "Are you sticking around for a drink?"

Friday drinks at the club are tempting, but not tonight. "I have something I need to do. Rain check?"

"I'll hold you to that."

Heading back to my desk, I shut everything down, collect my bag and coat and head out the door. Smiling as I step into the street, I inhale the aroma—kebabs, curry and a mix of culinary delights—and embrace the chaos of East London. Kim did good. Actually, life did good. After my forced holiday, three weeks of writing lists and researching places to live abroad—all of which were to prove to myself that I was doing things properly, because I already knew what I wanted—I called Kim.

London. That's where I wanted to be, and as luck would have it, the equivalent of my role in Nottingham was newly vacant in the Shoreditch office. You can take the girl out of East London, but it seems she will eventually find her way back. Shoreditch isn't my hometown, but it's a step up, and with a fifteen-minute walk to my flat, I don't even need to mess around with public transport.

Reaching my building, an old meat warehouse newly renovated into swanky flats that I can only afford thanks to Johnson's guilt money and the cut from the robbery given to me. The two dead men it belonged to have no use for it, after all.

Mum and Dad helped me move, and I've been here for a few days, filling my time hanging out with Dad and trying to persuade Tasha to move here with me. Days spent plucking up the courage to call the person I'm most desperate yet petrified to see.

That changes tonight.

The lift chimes, announcing that we've reached the fourth floor, and I walk out with a nervous spring in my step, only to stop in my tracks when I see a man leaning against my door. It appears that if you think about a person long enough, you manifest them.

"Breaking and entering?" I ask, my legs shaking as I make my way closer to him.

"I haven't broken a thing." Nate smiles, his confidence back where it belongs. I haven't seen him since that day in the pub, and I'm not sure which part of me is throbbing most.

"You need a key to get into this building."

He dangles a bunch of them in front of me in response and starts walking backwards to the next door along. Settling on one key, he unlocks it, switches on a light, and walks inside. "Home sweet home," he grins.

Following him in, I push the door closed. "Oh, sorry. I got my crimes mixed up… You're a stalker."

Laughing—always a beautiful sound—Nate tosses his keys on the side and stares me down, the heat in his eyes setting the butterflies in my stomach aflame. "I've never been happier than when I was living next door to you," he confesses.

"Ermm… your dad used to beat the shit out of you and your mum pissed your rent money up the wall."

Eyeing me like I'm his prey, Nate walks closer. "All true. But you made everything better." Stopping in front of me, the intoxicating scent of his aftershave surrounds me, and the heat from his body sends me into overdrive.

"I've been waiting…" His dominant side, the masked man who forced his way back into my life on full display.

"I've been busy."

"You've been hiding."

"That too," I laugh, feeling like the fifteen-year-old version of me the night she finally confessed her feelings.

Closing the tiny gap between us, he pushes a strand of hair behind my ear. "When I let you go off and think about your life, I made a huge error." His warm breath fanning my skin, the slight smell of nicotine that is usually off-putting, has the opposite effect on me when it comes from him.

"I let you go off and hide inside your mind, which…" He tilts his head to the side, mocking me. "Is usually filled with utter fucking nonsense, without making it crystal clear how I feel about you."

Pressing my body into his, I keep my hands by my sides, too afraid to let myself get lost in him. "You killed a man for me."

"Yes… But I never said the words, and the words matter. You need to hear them." Nate grips my hair, holding me in place, but in his eyes, I see he's waiting for permission.

Struggling to breathe, I force myself to speak, "Then say them now."

"Rachel… my Rachel. I'm going to give you the beautifully chaotic life you've always wanted. I'm going to fight for you, protect you, die in your place if I have to. When our lives come to an end, and you end up in heaven, I'll drag you into hell with me so we can continue to burn brightly together." Pausing, he waits for me to respond, laugh or tell him he's fucking crazy, none of which I do.

"You are my beginning, my end, my fucking forever, and I love you... I've always loved you."

Nate's lips graze mine, but he doesn't claim them because he needs to hear the words too. "I don't know how to compete with that declaration," I laugh, and he nips my bottom lip in response.

Taking a deep breath, I try to remember the speech I had planned for when I called him. "I came back to London because it's home, and I'm coming back to you because I can't live a half-life anymore. I can't function properly without my heart, and you stole it from me years ago." Wrapping my arms around him, I hold him close. "I'm not here to take it back, because it belongs with you, and so do I. You're it for me. Always have been, always will be. For better or worse, and an eternity burning in hell..." Laughing, I can't believe that sounds appealing, I finally confess, "I love you."

The End

Also by
Roxanna C Revell

Acknowledgments

So... dare I ask...? Did you love, loathe, like or decide this story was just one hefty dose of meh?

If you're in the love camp, it would be simply amazing if you could pop over to Amazon and Goodreads (and any other platform you fancy) and leave a review so that others can find their way to this world.

You wouldn't believe how long it took me to write this novella. It's my shortest published book, but getting it over the line took forever!

This novella started life with a maximum limit of 20,000 words and was supposed to be part of an anthology. Long story short, there were many bad reports coming from those involved in the first volume of the anthology, so I pulled out along with a few other authors I know.

But… I'd started the story, and while it was only a few thousand words, I already loved Nate and Rachel and wanted to see it through.

Why did it take so long, then? Life. That's all. The juggle of being a full-time working mum of two, whose energy and time are quite limited. I think not having a deadline didn't help either.

You're here, though, so I finally finished and published it.

Thank you for reading. Your support is much appreciated and gives me the kick I need to keep writing my darkly delicious stories.